TALES & DREAMS

Lost Time Academy: Book Two

G. BAILEY

TALES & DREAMS

G. BAILEY

Join <u>Bailey's Pack</u> on Facebook to stay in touch
with the author, find out what is coming out next
and any news!

www.gbaileyauthor.com

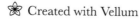 Created with Vellum

All the fairy tales are real, and now I can't escape them…even when they break my heart.

Madilynn Dormiens didn't know how dark the world really is, that is until the dark tales took it over. Death, pain and torment are the new motto of Lost Time Academy.

There is no place for love in this academy.

If the dark tales controlling the Lost Time Academy weren't difficult enough, The Tale brothers are out of control, and Quinton Frostan is causing trouble now that he is back in Madi's life.

The sort of trouble that will get them all killed.

Except Quinton is determined to make a big change, one that could bring someone they all want back…but the price of that change is too high. Too dangerous.

Love just might get them killed after all.

Even the Darkest Fairy Tales can fall in love…

18+ RH

Prologue

I bang my fists against his chest as thick tears stream down my cheeks. Once. Twice. Three times. I lose count of how many times I hit him before I fall to my knees, great sobs leaving my lips.

"You let him die! You just stood there as he was killed!" I scream at Quin. I can't get rid of the image of Sin on the cold grass, his body cold and empty of his soul. I see Quin kneel in front of me before he places a freezing cold finger under my chin and lifts my head to meet his blue eyes. There is so much guilt there, but I don't care. I just can't.

"It was Sin or you. If I stopped my uncle, you would both be dead. I hate myself more than you ever could for not being able to do anything," he gently tells me. I stay silent as he gets up and walks to the door. "I'm sorry." His words aren't enough, not for this, and they never could be. Sin didn't deserve to be the victim of that choice. I would have happily died to save him.

"Madi…" I jump, falling to the floor as I hear a familiar voice whisper my name. I sit up, frantically searching for who I think it was. I turn around as a raven flies across the field, swooping low and landing on the ground in front of me. I watch the raven as it steps closer and very quickly pecks my finger. I feel so numb from the shock of hearing that voice that I don't even cry out from the sudden pain. The raven flies away, and my finger drips blood onto the cold ground, but I feel empty and broken. The ravens are meant to protect me, that's what my Nan said…so why would it hurt me then?

How can Sin really be gone? That's the question that haunts me. I can't believe it, I won't.

"Sin?" I whisper. That was his voice, I'm sure of it. I'm not going crazy, I know I'm not. After a few seconds of nothing but silence and the chilling wind, I know I must have been wrong. Even that breaks my heart more to realise it. I hold my finger to stop the bleeding as I stand up, and just as I take a step to walk away, I hear it once more. This time, I'm sure it's him. I'd know Sin's voice anywhere.

"Madi…"

Chapter 1

I lie so very still, letting the ravens brush against my arms as they fall from the sky to lie next to me, their bodies and feathers keeping me warm. They keep falling all around me, almost like they want to comfort me, but I feel nothing but empty as I stare at the night sky above me. There are no stars, just a darkness that seems never-ending. I feel as cold as the grass under me and the air blowing around us. When the last raven falls, something inside me changes. I don't know what exactly it is, but I can't lie here anymore. I pull myself to my feet, even as my body screams at me not to. Emptiness is a nasty feeling; it takes you whole and leaves nothing left for you to cling to.

And I feel empty. I feel lost. I feel desperate…and only one person's name is on my lips. Oisin Tale.

The ravens are quiet as they lie on the ground, but I see they aren't dead as I look around at them. Their chests move up and down in rhythm with each other. I frown as I turn around, looking at the shape they are lying in.

It looks like an S.

S *for Sin...but the ravens can mourn all they want. I want revenge first and no more dreams. My dreams and powers were useless to really do anything when I needed them. When Sin needed me. The moment I think it, the ravens all sit up and swarm around me, blocking out any light as I fall back into them, letting the darkness take me.*

I groggily wake up, blinking at the daylight shining into my eyes as my hand goes straight to my head, feeling the hard lump there and a little dry blood. I quickly become aware I'm in my bed, looking up at the wooden boards above me where Tavvy's bed is. I run my hands over my dress, feeling the mud and how it is a little wet from the ice in places. As I lift my hands, I see the blood covering them, and a sob leaves my lips as I think of Sin's last moments. The room is eerily quiet as I wipe my tears away with the back of my hands and slide off the bed. I search around the room, seeing that Tavvy isn't here and neither is my book. Someone has taken Lane, but nothing else seems to be missing.

I freeze as I hear the sound of a door being unlocked, and I call my power to my hands. I don't care if it is Quin coming through that door. I'm not playing the victim, and I'm so furious with him. How could he just stand there while Sin died?

"Alright! Alright! No need to push me, you giant asshole!" I hear Tavvy protest as the door is opened and she practically falls into the room. I don't get to see who pushed her before the door is slammed shut and quickly locked. I wipe the dust away on my dress and fall in front of Tavvy, instantly reaching for the cut on her forehead that looks bad. Her dress is as ruined as mine, and her hair is partly loose whereas the rest is still held up by slides. When I meet her eyes, we both pause for second. The world just got incredibly scary, far more than it has ever been for us. If we thought Lost Time Academy was bad before, I'm certain it's going to be a whole new ball game now.

"Looks worse than it is. What happened to you?" Tavvy asks, her eyes widening at the blood on my hands and the state of my dress. I look down at the blood-stained dress and how the red looks so wrong against the blue. It shouldn't be there, because tonight should not have happened. The whole thing feels like a bad fairy tale that I read, only I can't close the book. I have to live it out and the raw pain that goes with it. I use all the strength I have to lift my head and take her hand tightly in mine. She only has to meet my teary eyes for a second to know something is really wrong. "Tell me, Madi. What happened?"

"Sin is dead." The words feel wrong as they leave my lips, and Tavvy pulls me tightly into her arms as I cry. He is really gone. Just gone, and there is no magical way to bring him back to me.

"Bastards. We will kill them all for this. I promise you the dark tales will not win this war. I can't promise you anything other than the fact we are going to fight to survive this," she firmly tells me, tears streaming down her dirt- and blood-covered cheeks, leaving clear streaks.

"Quin is one of them," I whisper, and it doesn't sound right to even say it out loud. Quinton, the boy I grew up with. The boy who loved the Tale brothers like the siblings he never had. And he betrayed them all the moment he decided to let Sin die and not help him.

"Your ex-boyfriend? The human?" she asks,

confused. I know how she feels. I hardly even believe it yet. I keep seeing Quin standing there, looking so different. So cold and empty, just like the powers he has. They must have done a complete personality transplant when he got those powers, because the Quin I knew, the Quin I loved, wouldn't have stood there. He wouldn't have knocked me out because someone told him to, either. Quinton used to be a good person… and now it seems none of that boy is left.

"Isn't human. He is a dark tale," I whisper, wiping more tears away. "He stood there as Sin was killed. Sin was like a brother to him, and he didn't care."

"Fuck," she mutters in as much shock as I am. "The dark tales have full control of the academy. They are locking everyone in their rooms for now. I saw a girl called Venny, one of Ella's close friends, tried to attack a dark tale. They killed her like it was nothing and burned her body away. That's the new rules now; they kill and do not care. Our instinct is to attack them, and my skin is itching to do just that."

I find it odd that's how she feels about them, because other than how angry and upset I am with Quinton, I didn't feel a natural instinct to kill him. I'm considering it now though. He doesn't deserve to live when he let Sin go. It seems like a million memories flash through my head of Oisin and Quinton, and how they were best friends. I remember them riding their bikes down to my house, and they were always laughing together by the time I got outside. I even saw them hug once, when Quinton had a hard time at home with his mother, and he was really upset. Sin was always there for Quinton, actually more than the others. He always had his back...and Quinton let him get stabbed in the back like he was nothing to him.

"I didn't want to kill Quin," I tell her, looking down at my blood-stained hands. Dirt and blood nearly cover all of the pale skin. I look to my academy symbol, where dots of blood have dripped through the mark. It makes it look more sinister than usual.

"Really?" she asks me, and I have a funny feeling she has said it more than once before I've noticed. "Not one stabby thought?"

"Not until he let Sin be killed, no," I reply, realising that we are still sitting on the floor and need to stand up. If we keep sitting here, we might as well raise a flag that says the dark tales have beaten us and won. Sin wouldn't want me to give up, but it's hard to even think of him without crying. I get up first and hold a hand out for Tavvy to get up too. "I don't want to talk about Quin anymore. He doesn't deserve a moment of my pain. I need to see the Tale brothers, and that is what I'm going to focus on. They have to know what happened to Sin. All of it, down to the last difficult detail," I say, because it's the right thing to do. I know they will go after Quin and the man that killed Sin, but first of all, we need to mourn. We need to say goodbye, no matter how wrong it is, because Sin was seventeen. He was my age, and it's no age to die at all.

I don't feel like a seventeen-year-old, and I really haven't for a long time. The world took what was left of my childhood innocence and crushed it like a bug when I was taken here and left to face the real world without my parents there to hold my hand. Hell, I really miss them, and I wish my mum was here to hug me, to explain how to grieve Sin. How to cope with Quinton being back. How to stop my heart from feeling like it's been torn into a million pieces.

"I don't think we can do anything until they let us out. We play by their rules for now, and then we make a plan," Tavvy says, placing her hands on her hips and nodding her head, like this is the best plan there is. It's better than sitting on the floor, crying and feeling beaten, I guess.

"What are the dark tales' rules?" I ask her. "We have been told they are evil, and everything they have done so far suggests just that."

"Nothing good, that's for sure," she replies, and she places her hand on her head, wincing. "This stings. Do we have any first aid stuff?"

"Yeah, my mum packed me a small kit actually," I reply, and I just realise I have my phone as I think of where the kit is. "I have my phone!"

"That's good. We need to tell the tales community what has happened, Madi," Tavvy says. "Maybe they can send help or tell us what to do."

"Do you know your parents' number? I'm going to call mine first and let them know," I answer, because I don't want to call the tales community first. If they could take back the academy, they would be here. I know it, and so does Tavvy. We are on our own here, and the adults who are meant to protect us won't be doing that.

"I have it written down somewhere. You call them while I look for it," she says as I squat down and pull my phone out from a box under my bed, next to the first aid kit, which I hand to Tavvy. She starts cleaning her head and sticking a plaster over the cut for now as I turn my phone on. I frown at the ten percent battery I have left. It won't last too long, so I need to make every second count. I quickly call my parents, and my heart feels like it's beating fast every moment I wait for them to answer. *Please, please let them be alive.*

"Madi? Please say you are okay?" My mum's frantic voice pleads down the phone, and I let out a sigh of pure, perfect relief. They are alive, and mum sounds alright. They know Lost Time Academy has been taken, but that is worrying. If they know, then there is a good chance no one is coming to rescue us because they can't. I thought that anyway, but hearing evidence of it is a totally other thing altogether.

"I'm okay. Well, not okay, but alive at least," I tell her, and she cries down the phone as I hear it being taken off her.

"What have those bastards done to you?" my dad growls, and I hear him quietly tell mum that they need to get to the academy somehow and rescue me. Mum tells him it isn't possible, even with the one key they have. Other parents have apparently been trying to get in, and the keys don't work anymore. "Madi, I will find a way——"

"Oisin is dead. We are locked in our room with no clue what is going on and...Quinton is a dark tale," I blurt out all the worst things first, hoping that somehow it's going to make things easier in this conversation. The more I say those words, the more they feel real, and I feel closer to the edge of breaking down. *Sin is dead. Quinton is evil. The Lost Time Academy is lost.*

"What?" my dad's voice is shocked, whereas my mum is crying her eyes out in the background as my hand shakes, and I nearly drop the phone. The harsh beep of the low battery snaps me out of it. I can breakdown later; this might be the last time I can talk to my parents for a long time. I need to make it last. I need to remember their voices. Dad is shocked into silence, I think, as I hear the phone being passed somewhere, and then there is a very welcome voice I didn't expect.

"Now my sweet Madi, the dead never leave us, remember that. Have the ravens been around yet?" my grandmother says, her voice sweet and familiar. It reminds me of all the fairy tales she used to read to me as a child. It reminds me of the cookies she would always bake for when I was staying over. My grandmother somehow makes me feel comforted, even when comfort was not something I was expecting.

"The ravens are always in my dreams. I saw the future in my dreams, I just didn't know it," I admit to her. "I'm meant to have sleep powers only. How the hell did I see the moment before Sin died in my sleep? Why do the ravens haunt me like I'm a long lost friend of theirs, yet I can't use them to actually help me?"

"The ravens protect our family, and everything will come out in the end. You trust in them, sweetie. They guide both the living and the dead," she tells me. "They are guides, but you have the blood of the ravens, Madilynn. Sleep maybe your strongest descendant line, but it is not your only one."

"Grandma, I don't think the ravens can help me or Sin anymore. He is gone, and I l-loved him," my voice cracks, and I try to hide the pain I'm feeling from her, but it doesn't work. There is always that one person you can't hide the truth from, no matter how much you try. It doesn't work because their voice alone cracks something deep down inside of you.

"Oh my sweet Madi. We live in a world of

pure magic, and death is not always final. Remember that, and go now. We are going into hiding while the tales fight the war, like many families are. The dark tales won't hurt you young ones, and that means they will not see you coming to beat them. They want to groom you to be on their side. Be careful what you believe, and be careful of your heart. Dark tales don't fall in love, and if they do, it's all or nothing." The call ends after her ominous words, and I hand it to Tavvy, who I can see is worried about me. There is no place for love when you can only think of death.

And the dead don't come back.

Chapter 2

"One step at a time, Madi," Tavvy keeps telling me that after she stated we needed to get out of the ruined dresses and into new clothes. She said that we needed to wipe the blood off my hands and try to at least do the normal things, even when there is nothing normal about this situation. I can't think of anything but Sin...and making a plan to kill the man who took his life. I can't do much but spend every second trying not to break down, to fall into a pit of tears and never stop crying. That's what I want to do, but I try to keep my head up and focus on finding out who killed Sin, so I can tell his brothers a name. Quin knows who it was, and I'm not going to rest until he tells me the name.

My other thoughts stray to the Tale brothers and how they are coping with everything...or if they know at all. I hug my legs closer to my chest as I sit on the floor, with Tavvy sat behind me as she gently French plaits my hair for me, careful to avoid the lump and cut on my head. I don't feel the pain though; it's nothing compared to how I feel inside.

"I need to get out of this room," I tell her, because being trapped in here all day has just made things a million times worse.

"I feel that on so many levels. I don't like that we have no clue what is going on," she replies as I feel her finishing the plait off and tying it.

"How is your head feeling?" I ask her, turning my head back to see her bandage has a little blood showing but, considering we didn't have much to work with, it will do.

"Sore, but I'm good," she replies as I stand up. I smooth down my oversized grey top that is tucked into my sweatpants. I'm not dressing up for these monsters. Tavvy quickly comes to my side as we hear the door being unlocked, and seconds later, it is pushed open. The man standing in the doorway is a dark tale. He is hidden under a cloak with a long black hood, so I can't see much else about him other than he is taller than me. I can sense a dislike for him, but I don't have that urge to attack him like I can see Tavvy wants to from the way her pupils are wide and alert, and her body is tense. I grab her arm to stop her walking forward, especially considering the man has a long spear in his hand, and the tip of the spear is glowing with grey energy that almost looks like smoke.

"Out. Now," he commands in a deep voice that makes me shiver.

"Where are we meant to go?" I ask him, though I can't see his face under the long hood. I'm sure it's purposely done to make him seem more frightening.

"The dining hall for your first academy assembly," he informs me. "Now move before I am forced to make you." I focus on the fact he claims he would be forced and not that he wants to cause us pain.

"Fine," I reply, grabbing Tavvy's arm tighter to force her to walk out of the room with me. She does, though I can feel that she really doesn't want to do anything but kill that dude. I don't exactly blame her disliking all the dark tales that have taken over the academy, but he hasn't done anything to us.

"Just chill. It's not worth dying over right at this moment," I whisper to her, and she looks at me and takes a deep breath as she briefly closes her eyes before we carry on walking. We stop when we see another hooded man standing outside Ella's room, and Ella walks out, pausing when she notices me. Ella's red hair is a mess, and her face is red and blotchy from crying. Instead of revealing clothing, Ella has a black top and black leggings on. Overall, I just about recognise her, and I instantly want to comfort her, even though we aren't exactly friends.

Without another word, she turns and walks with her hooded man following right behind her. I glance at Tavvy, and we both don't need to say we are concerned for Ella. I mean, we aren't what I'd even consider friends, but I guess some part of me does like her. You know, when she isn't after my guys. Even then, everything has become so much more than arguing over guys and things like that. Now we are concerned for our lives, and that makes me want to keep Ella alive to fight on my side at least, even if we don't like each other.

The academy is silent, bar the footsteps of the

students being led to the dining hall. I glance around, but I don't see the Tale brothers at all in the mix of students. We head down the stairs, where five hooded dark tales are standing at the sides. I make a mental note that none of the dark tales have weapons like the one walking behind us. Also, I notice the clip in the middle of their cloaks is a wolf sitting on an eye in a circle, the very opposite of the mark on my wrist with the cat on the moon. I hate cats and their love of attacking me, but I'm thinking I should be more scared of the wolf at the moment. Shame, because I like the wolves in the stories.

We follow the crowd into the dining room, where everyone is sitting down on the black chairs that are in rows on either side of a path through the middle. Big black curtains are pulled across the front of the room, so we can't see what they want to show us. The room is eerily quiet, even with this many people in it, and there is just a certain feel of tension that I can't explain. Snow lightly falls from the ceiling, though there are no clouds, and I'm certain that Quin is causing the snow. I'm not sure if I even want to see him, because I'm scared of what I'm going to do.

. . .

*H*e let Sin die.

I slide into the seat next to Ella, who doesn't look my way as she harshly wipes tears away from her eyes, looking so angry as she does. Like her tears are an insult to her. I'm sure it's the death of her friend that is upsetting her, and well, everything that is going on. Before I've really thought about it, I place my hand on hers and squeeze it gently. She sharply looks to me as I take my hand away, and she nods once.

"They killed my parents. My aunt is locked up and will be killed soon, I bet. Then they killed my friend because she wouldn't do what they asked. What is left to hope for?" she whispers, though I feel like her words get the attention of everyone around us because they look our way ever so slightly.

"Us. We will avenge those who are gone when they least expect it. They will pay for this," I whisper back, and she stares at me intently. I could say I'm so sorry, but those words mean nothing in the grand scheme of things. Sorry won't bring them back or make her feel better.

Quin said he was sorry to me as I stared at Sin's dead body on the cold ground, and I know it means nothing. Ella smirks at me before lifting her head high and looking much more like the badass bitch I know and sometimes dislike.

"That we will. I'm on your side, Madi," she says, using my name for once. It's almost strange not to hear her call me new girl. I look to Tavvy, who is staring at the stage like everyone else is as the last of the students come into the room.

"Have you seen the Tale brothers?" I whisper to Tavvy, and she shakes her head, looking as concerned as I am. They already killed one of them like they were nothing, and I know they wouldn't think twice before doing that again. I can't lose any of them, not like Sin. My heart is crushed as it is.

The doors to the dining room slam shut behind the last person to come into the room, and the black hooded guys stand in a line in front of the door and down the walls. The one with the spear stands right in the middle of them. I was right, he is important, so why is he watching us and not someone more dangerous like the Tale brothers? The curtains move ever so slightly before a man steps out, clapping his hands together once with a large smile on his face as I rest back in my chair.

"Welcome, Lost Time Academy students," he says, lowering his hands and holding them behind his back as he stops. I recognise his voice though. He was the one that killed Sin, I know it. His hair is white, pure white, and it almost reflects against his bright blue eyes. His suit is black, and parts of it are covered in frost like he doesn't have control over his powers. They are like Quin's, I'm coming to realise. Ice and snow. Cold and deadly, just like their actions. "My name is Rueben Frostan, the current king of the dark tales and *your* new king. I know you are not used to these terms, but be assured we will help you accommodate to the new rules we are setting."

"By murdering those who disagree, he means," Ella mutters under her breath.

"Now, there will be big changes to Lost Time Academy. For one, you have new teachers and new classes. As you leave, you are expected to accept your new schedule and cloak. The cloaks must be worn at all times, and there is high penalty for skipping classes," he states, and I would almost want to laugh if I weren't sure he was deadly serious.

"What penalty? You've already taken over. Why not kill us?" a guy I don't know well asks, standing up. Rueben narrows his eyes on the guy, who holds his head high and doesn't back down. Roger sits at his side, and he tries to make his friend sit down by grabbing his jacket and tugging.

"I'm very glad you asked, my new friend," Rueben remarks, sounding very friendly, but I don't believe it. He claps his hands once as he steps to the side. The curtains slowly fall back, revealing a large cage made from ice spikes. Cries and gasps fill my ears when I see Miss Noa in the cage, with dozens of spikes of ice pressing her to the back of the cage ice wall. Blood had poured onto the floor, freezing before it could go anywhere. She isn't breathing, by the looks of her, and I'm speechless to say anything. *I'm sorry we couldn't save her.* I look to the left, where Quinton is standing, his arms crossed with a neutral expression as students gasp and cry. He isn't wearing one of those cloaks, so he is important somehow to Rueben. They also share the same ice power, so they must be related somehow, that is the only thing that makes sense.

Quinton's eyes move to me, and he holds my

gaze as I glare at him before looking back at Rueben as he starts talking once the cries die down. "Every week, I will be placing a new teacher in here until they all die. When I run out of teachers for my cage, I will be needing new replacements. The replacements will be found with the students that break the rules, so I suggest you all learn to behave in the new world you have found yourself in." No one says a word, because what can you really say to that utter madness that he just said? He looks as crazy as he clearly is.

"One more thing before you are all dismissed. The Tale brothers are missing. Anyone that has information on them, come to me. There will be a big reward and a very happy future for the person that brings the brothers to me." Rueben looks at me the entire time he speaks and relief fills my chest. *They escaped somehow.* I know they wouldn't come for me straight away, not until I'm alone and it is safe. It's not been safe yet.

And instead of giving him what he wants, I smile as I stand up straight. They don't have the Tale brothers, and I have nothing to lose. If they wanted me dead, I would be already, and I can't just sit here silently. This is madness, utter madness.

"Yes...well, I am not sure of your name?" Rueben states.

"It's Madilynn Dormiens. You said we were dismissed, right?" I ask. "I'd like to leave. It's a bit chilly in here for my liking."

"Everyone can leave except for you, Miss Madilynn Dormiens. We need to have a little chat," he says, and everyone gets up after he claps his hands.

"I can stay," Tavvy says, looking nervously at me, and Ella stays still as students push past us to escape the hall.

"No, I can handle this. Go with Ella, I'll catch up. He already killed Sin; he can't scare me anymore," I tell her, and I look at Ella, asking her to make Tavvy leave with only a look. Ella's breath hitches because she must not have known about Sin. She wipes a tear away and places her hand on my arm for a second, squeezing tightly before letting go. I have to swallow down the emotion that burns in my throat. I can't cry now. I can't show Rueben any weakness. Ella hooks her arm in Tavvy's and makes her walk out of the room, which I'm thankful for. I wait until the room is empty except for Rueben, Quin and the man with a spear, who closes the doors before I look back at Rueben who is patiently waiting.

"It would be a pleasure to have a little chat. You can start by telling me why the fuck you killed Oisin Tale, and then I can tell you how I'm going to kill you for touching him at all," I growl, curling my hands into fists and feeling my power bubbling up without me calling for it.

"I like you," he chuckles before rubbing his chin and looking to Quinton as he comes to his side. The look Quin gives me suggests I should have kept my mouth shut. I don't regret saying it though. "I can see why you love this one."

"He doesn't love me," I snap, looking back as the man with the spear steps closer. "Love isn't that fucked up."

"Dear Miss Madilynn Dormiens, you will not hurt me," he tells the man before placing those creepy blue eyes on me. "We are going to be friends, you and I."

"Unless you think friends are people that want to kill each other, no we are not," I sarcastically respond, crossing my arms. Has this man being drinking the Kool Aid or something?

"Mr. Newman told me all about your powers.

See, we grew up together, and he was a good friend. Much like you and Quin are in *some* respects. Though I did kill him once I found out all the information I wanted. A good tale like him could not be fully trusted," he explains to me in a matter of fact way. I'm kind of relieved he killed the disturbing Mr. Newman, especially if he told Rueben everything he wanted to know. I'm also realising more and more about how mad Rueben is; he killed his own friend. "I am very interested in pushing your dormant powers further, and every Sunday morning, I want you to come here for a private lesson."

"I'd rather not," I'm quick to shut that idea up. I couldn't imagine anything worse than private lessons with the monster that killed Sin.

"I wasn't asking, Madilynn. If you do not obey me, it will not just be your boyfriend I will kill. I see you have friends in my grasp, and if they are not motivation enough, I will send a hunt out for your parents," he says, walking over to me as I try not to shake with anger. "Until Sunday, Madilynn. My personal guard will be keeping a close eye on you for now." I don't have to look behind me to know he means the spear dude is my new stalker. I turn my head back and watch as Rueben leaves the room, and the spear dude shuts the door.

"I will watch Madilynn for a bit and return her to her room. Why don't you get her a cloak and a schedule while we talk?" Quinton tells the man.

"Yes, sir," the dude dutifully says before leaving the room, and it's silent as I look back to Quinton.

"Let's talk outside," Quinton suggests and walks to the doors outside without waiting for my reply. I follow him out of the building and over to where he stands on the grass courtyard which is empty. If I look over the field, I will be able to see the spot where Sin died.

I walk straight up to Quin, who turns to face me, opening his mouth to talk. I don't want to hear it.

"I'm so—" That is all he gets to say before I punch him hard in the face.

 e deserved it.

Chapter 3

"I guess I deserved that," he says, rubbing his cheek where it is already swelling. My knuckles feel like they will bruise for that, but I don't care. He deserved it and so much more, and I like knowing he is hurting. *He let Sin die.*

I bang my fists against his chest as thick tears stream down my cheeks. Once. Twice. Three times. I lose count of how many times I hit him before I fall to my knees, great sobs leaving my lips.

"You let him die! You just stood there as he was killed!" I scream at Quin. I can't get rid of the image of Sin on the cold grass, his body cold and empty of his soul. I see Quin kneel in front of me before he places a freezing cold finger under my chin and lifts my head to meet his blue eyes. There is so much guilt there, but I don't care. I just can't.

"It was Sin or you. If I stopped my uncle, you would both be dead. I hate myself more than you ever could for not being able to do anything," he gently tells me. I stay silent as he gets up and walks to the door. "I'm sorry." His words aren't enough, not for this, and they never could be. Sin didn't deserve to be the victim of that choice. I would have happily died to save him.

"Madi..." I jump, falling to the floor as I hear a familiar voice whisper my name. I sit up, frantically searching for who I think it was. I turn around as a raven flies across the field, swooping low and landing on the ground in front of me. I watch the raven as it steps closer and very quickly pecks my finger. I feel so numb from the shock of hearing that voice that I don't even cry out from the sudden pain. The raven flies away, and my finger drips blood onto the cold ground, but I feel empty and broken. The ravens are meant to protect me, that's what my Nan said...so why would it hurt me then?

How can Sin really be gone? That's the question that haunts me. I can't believe it, I won't.

"Sin?" I whisper. That was his voice, I'm sure of it. I'm not going crazy, I know I'm not. After a few seconds of nothing but silence and the chilling wind, I know I must have been wrong. Even that breaks my heart more to realise it. I hold my finger to stop the bleeding as I stand up, and just as I take a step to walk away, I hear it once more. This time, I'm sure it's him. I'd know Sin's voice anywhere.

"Madi…"

I spin around, a cry escaping my lips when I see a version of Sin right in front of me, as clear as day. His body is almost see-through, though it still looks like him so much that it hurts. His blonde hair almost looks white like this, and his silver eyes are so bright that it hurts to look at them. I step closer, seeing how the ghost figure of his body is deathly still. It's just a reminder that he is gone, and I have no clue what this is in front of me.

"Sin?" I whisper again. Tears drip into my mouth as I take one more step closer. I slowly reach a shaky hand out to touch him, to see if he is real, but his voice stops me.

"Don't. I'm not really here, at least the physical side of me isn't," Sin tells me. My chest hurts, feeling like it's burning in pain as I stare at him. This is cruel. It's like death itself is teasing me.

"How are you here? I watched you die," I manage to whisper.

"Death can't take my soul, Madi. I promised it to you a long time ago," he tells me. A pain-filled gasp leaves my lips as more tears roll down my face, and I taste the saltiness of them on my lips. I'm sure he is here to say goodbye and break my heart when he goes. "Don't cry. I can't touch you, hold you and tell you it's all going to be okay. Please…just please don't cry."

"I want you back. I never got a chance to tell you—"

"Don't say it. You can't love a ghost, Madi. You need to find a way to be okay," he pleads with me, and I step closer. I feel colder near him like this, and it's like he wants me to move away.

"I'm not okay, though. I never will be without you," I honestly say. My fingers itch to try and touch him, despite his warning. "And you can tell me not to love you, but that won't stop how I feel, Sin."

"I know," he says, smiling sadly, and his eyes

drift over to the door. "I must leave, but I'm always here, Madi. I'm always around…for now at least." Sin fades away into nothing, literally nothing, but it feels like he took another part of my very soul with him. I sob for a second as I reach a hand out into the air where he was, but there is nothing there. It makes me think I might have lost my mind somewhere along the way. *Did I really just see Sin here?*

"Miss Dormiens, you are requested to return to your room," the spear guys says as he walks out of the door that Sin was looking at, his heavy boots slamming across the gravel.

"What is your name? Or should I keep calling you spear guy?" I say, and I can feel his smile, even though I can't see it under his hood. Something about him gets my attention, and I'm not sure what it is. I want to try and be friends with him anyway, considering his new job is to stalk me.

"My name is Warren. I would prefer you call me that instead of *spear guy*," he sourly replies. I nod and walk over to him with a smile, seeing he has a plastic bag in his hand which he hands to me. "Your new cloak and schedule for classes. Breakfast will be brought to your room at six a.m.

every morning, and first class starts at eight thirty a.m."

"Is there food in there? I'm pretty hungry," I admit, being they haven't fed us and I'm trying to avoid going back to my room because Tavvy is going to have a million questions I don't have the answer to. I want to stay out here…just in case he comes back. Which he might do.

"No, but I will order food to be served to you," he replies.

"And *all* the students while you are at it. I can't be the only one hungry," I say, crossing my arms.

"You're rather bossy, you know that?" he mutters.

"You have a lot to learn, Warren," I chuckle before walking through the door into the academy. My smile doesn't last long when reality soon hits home, and my body aches to go back outside where Sin was. That can't be the last time I see him…I'm not ready to say goodbye to him yet. I doubt I ever truly will be.

I'm trapped in an academy full of dark tales, and it looks like no one is going to be able to help me. I stare around at the entrance hall, which is being redesigned with everything black, by the looks of it, by some dark tales in large hoods. It's almost funny to see guys that are dressed like Grim Reapers painting walls. We head up the stairs and to the right, straight to my room, where Warren stays outside as I shut the door on him. Arms wrap around me almost instantly, and I turn, smiling as I hug Tavvy back.

"I was worried! What happened with——" she stops as we both hear a small buzzing before there is a white flash in the room. A portal burns into existence, and seconds later, Noah steps out. His eyes are bloodshot, his gaze is serious, and I just know he knows about Sin without saying a word. Tavvy links her hand with mine as I stare at Noah. I don't know what to say and neither does he. I'm just happy to see him alive and well. He doesn't say a word, he just holds out his hand, and I walk to him, taking it before letting him pull me and Tavvy through the portal.

Chapter 4

"So this is where you've been?" Tavvy questions as she gapes at the other dimension, Knox's secret hiding place, which is not that secret at all now by the looks of it. The last time I was here, there was just Knox's hut, a little pool and not much else in a big forest. Now there are dozens of huts spread all around Knox's in the middle, with people walking around. The biggest of the huts is to our right, and it's one massive building. "Who are all these people?"

"The Masters and what is left of the council. We got everyone we could out before they destroyed the building and the entire tales town," Noah explains, even though he sounds very tired, and he looks just as bad. Noah usually has golden skin, but being here, he looks very pale, and his soft brown hair is messy, matching the beard he is starting to grow. Noah has the same clothes on from the party, the handsome tux which is now covered in dust, burns and holes. The tie is missing, and the white shirt has a tear down the middle of it. They must have been here all day, and it looks like Knox has been doing some renovation at least. That gives me hope he isn't too lost in grief.

"How many got out?" Tavvy asks. "I'm so glad my parents are hiding in the human world and they are safe, but I know a lot more couldn't have been."

"About one hundred got out, so we lost well over seven hundred men, women and children. They killed them all," Noah answers, and I tense. "Are your parents doing the same, Madi? When we realised that you weren't with…that we didn't know where you were but we expected that Sin was keeping you safe. We went to your parents' house, but it was empty, so we assumed they are alright."

"Yeah," I answer, as we just stare at each other. I want to throw my arms around him and kiss away the pain in his eyes. He looks tired with the world, with the pain it causes and, right in this moment, I do not blame him.

"I'm going to look around," Tavvy awkwardly says, clearing her throat and walking to the hut.

"I'm so, so sorry about Sin," I say, but my voice comes out like a whisper. "I miss him so much already. I miss him so much that it doesn't seem real that he's really gone." Noah pulls me into his arms, tightening them around me as we both figure out how to cope with the loss. I don't think I ever will learn how to cope with it, but here we are. Noah eventually pulls away, and I lift my hand, wiping his wet cheeks.

"I need your help," he asks me, reaching up and tucking some strands of my hair behind my ear.

"Anything," I immediately answer. There isn't anything I wouldn't do for them.

"I need your help with Knox. He is out of control," Noah admits. "I've tried reasoning with him or just getting him to think logically, but that didn't work."

"Where is Tobias?" I ask, because if Knox is out of control, I can't imagine how Tobias is coping. He never takes change or grief well.

"Tobias has disappeared into the forest, and

we haven't seen him since we got here," he explains, which is more than concerning.

"What do you mean Knox is out of control, then?" I ask. "One Tale brother at a time."

"His powers are strongly tied to his emotions —" Noah stops, nodding his head to the building Tavvy just went into, where fire is suddenly pouring out of the roof, along with water and lightning. Holy Batman, that looks scary.

I'm running towards the building before Noah can stop me, but I hear him following me anyway. I push the door open and see the large room we are in is slowly being destroyed by Knox. He doesn't look like my Knox though; he looks like a shadow of the man I know. His hair is all over his face, almost covering his eyes, and his clothes are a total mess. Death does that to a person...and Sin was his twin.

Everyone in the room backs away from him. The fire, water, air and even lightning blasts out of his hands in his anger and grief.

Noah grabs my arm to try and stop me when I take a step forward. He can't though.

Knox Tale doesn't frighten me.

I walk straight to him, through the elements that brush close to me but never quite touch.

"Knox," I only have to whisper his name, and he snaps out of it.

Anger turns to pain in a matter of moments, and Knox falls to his knees. And I fall right there with him. I wrap my arms around his chest, holding him tightly as he holds me back just as strongly. It's hard to breathe as I hear him sob into my neck, his grief is overwhelming, and he is shaking from it. I hate seeing Knox like this. I've never seen him so…broken. The worst part is that I have no clue how to fix it.

I look behind me at Tavvy, Noah and the bunch of people I don't know except for two. The Tale brothers' parents. They stand there like statues, staring at me holding their son who is breaking down. I want to throw something at them, make them show some sort of emotion for him. For Sin. Other than the thick dark rings under Mrs. Tale's eyes, indicating she hasn't been sleeping, I wouldn't suspect anything is wrong. Mr. Tale is a little different though; his clothes are wrinkled and his eyes red from crying. His hands are in fists at his side, but he doesn't move to comfort Knox. That should be a parent's first instinct: to comfort their child after a great loss. Not just watch him like a spectator at an event.

"What did you say to him this time?" Noah asks his mother, who just stares at us for a second longer before turning and walking away. Noah rubs his face and looks to the crowd. "Everyone out. The show is over!" Noah's voice echoes, and everyone quickly makes their way out, including Tavvy, with Noah closing the door behind her after she flashes me a worried smile.

"How did it happen?" Knox asks me, his voice is hoarse and rugged. The pain in his tone is hard to hear. How do I tell him any of it? I know I need to. I planned to, but now that I'm here, the words don't want to leave my lips. They are frozen. Knox pulls back, placing his hands on my shoulders as Noah gets to us, and he looks at me. Those dark silver eyes look so hollow now. He is still so beautiful, but it's a dark sort of beauty now. Everything has changed.

"We ran to the forest to escape, but—" I pause. "Quinton was there. He is a dark tale."

"Did he kill my brother?" Knox coldly asks, but he doesn't look shocked about Quinton at all. He just wants to know who took Sin's life, which I understand. "Did he freeze him so he wasn't look-ing? Did he make an ice sword and stab him or something? I've seen the wound, I know it was ice, so don't protect him. Tell me."

"You knew he was a dark tale?" I ask him, and his hands tighten on my shoulders.

"Did he kill Sin, Madi?" Knox growls back at me, keeping his eyes locked on me. I know he wants to push me away because I can see straight through his anger and bullshit. I know him too well, and he hates that right now.

"No, it was his uncle, Rueben Frostan. He is some sort of king of the dark tales, and I guess that makes Quin the prince," I reply, and Knox clenches his jaw before standing up. I stand with him, grabbing his hand when he tries to storm away from me.

"I need to be alone," he states. "Alone means without you, Madi."

"No, you don't. I think you need some sleep, if I'm being honest," I suggest, but before he can protest, I slam my hand over his face after calling my powers, and he falls to the floor like a brick. I cringe at the fact that must have hurt him, but I knew he would never let me do it otherwise. Noah walks to my side, placing his hand on the middle of my back as he looks down at Knox with me.

"Good call. He needs to rest," Noah says.

"I hate doing that to him," I admit, but he would have just pushed me away and said things he didn't mean. He isn't thinking straight, and I can't take anything he said to heart, even if all I want Knox to do is hold me and protect me. For now, I need to protect him instead.

"Most the time, we hate doing the right thing. The right thing is never easy, remember?" he says, smiling at me, but I see the pain in his eyes. He looks tired too.

"Any chance I could convince you to sleep for a bit?" I ask.

"We need to call a meeting about what the next step is," he says, rubbing his face with his hands. "Then I promise to rest." I nod, because what else can I say to that? If we don't have a plan, we are going to be stuck in here while the rest of our world burns.

Chapter 5

"That is so weird how it fixes itself," Tavvy comments from my side as we watch the roof of the room Knox destroyed put itself back together and almost heal itself in a way. Tavvy says she picked a flower outside, and the flower just grew itself back as she watched. All magic must have some price though, and this is a lot of magic. I need to speak to Knox and make sure he can handle it. I don't know exactly how this place works, but it can't be free. Nothing good is free.

"Noah says everything here can only be changed by Knox, and so everything goes back to the way he made it unless he wants it changed. The water is endless, and the fruit always reappears seconds after you pick it. In reality, everyone could stay here until they die, and it would be perfect," I explain the little I do know thanks to Noah.

"But everyone back at the academy and the world would be in danger," she replies, and I don't have a clue what to say back to her. She is right of course, because staying here wouldn't make the rest of the world be at peace. Noah steps in front of the crowd of people who stand just behind us, and each one of them feels like they are nervous. His parents move to stand at his side, his mum keeping her eyes fixed on me.

"Thank you for coming here so quickly for a meeting. As you know, the tales community has fallen and, with it, many people we all loved. We all miss them, but we must look to the future now to save what we have left," Noah says, and I'm super proud of him for being the one to stand up alone in front of them all and say it. I can see how Noah feels without him saying a word. He feels like he has lost more than just one brother. Tobias is off god knows where, and Knox isn't coping with the world enough to wake up right now. If Noah doesn't make a stand, then who else is going to? The two Masters that are left, in my opinion, don't seem to want to take control and save everyone.

"How can we do that? The tales' army was destroyed protecting the community, and we have nothing left," a man asks, stepping forward. He has big horns instead of ears, and the horns stretch up into his hair before sticking up in the air. Noah doesn't look like he has a clue how to answer that, and when it becomes clear his parents aren't going to step in, I have to say something. I have to do something.

"You have us. We are from the academy. My name is Madilynn Dormiens, and this is Octavia Bell. I can get close enough to the dark tales' leader, Rueben Frostan, to kill him," I say, because it's the truth. It would take a while to get him to trust me, but I think being at the academy and behaving would eventually get me where I need to be. "Or I can get him alone for the Tale brothers to open a portal and drag him here then kill him. Either way, I'm in the academy and the best chance we have. I'm powerful enough to defend myself and more than willing to take the risk."

"You think he would be so easily tricked or killed?" Mrs. Tale asks and laughs. "He killed all the Masters and nearly us, but we just about escaped with our lives due to Knox and his power. A girl like you wouldn't stand a chance against him."

"He asked me to come to him every Sunday for private lessons. I'm close to his heir, someone he trusts. I know I can get them to trust me, and then I can finish this war," I say. "And, no offense, Mrs. Tale, I don't see you volunteering to save us all." Mrs. Tale shakes her head like I'm a silly, clueless girl, but she doesn't say anything. It's Noah that looks at me next like I'm mad.

"No," Noah says, shaking his head. "That is too dangerous. You are not going back to that academy alone."

"She won't be alone; I will be there. None of the students in the academy want the dark tales to rule, and they will help us too," Tavvy says, stepping to my side. I nod once at her, appreciating that she is doing this.

"I don't think putting our entire future in the hands of a—"

"Mother, enough. The Masters failed, you failed and it cost Oisin his damn life. Do not insult Madilynn for coming up with the only plan on the table right now. We don't have a choice here, and the last thing I want to do is send the woman I love back to that academy, but here we are," Noah snaps at her. I'm shocked silent because that is the first time Noah has said he loves me, and I really wish it wasn't in a conversation with his crazy mother. Still, I love that he defended me like that. I know it must have been hard for him to do that. Noah and the rest of the Tale brothers have always believed in the Masters and the plan they had for the future.

Mrs. Tale walks off in a huff, with Mr. Tale quickly following behind her. I mouth "thank you" to Noah, who smiles at me before clapping his hands to stop the quiet whispers spreading through the small crowd.

"I'm sorry about that. You are all dismissed," Noah says, and the crowd awkwardly starts to leave except for Tavvy, who stays as I walk to Noah. He tugs me into his arms, holding me closely to him as he presses a kiss on my head.

"Don't take any crazy risks. I mean it," Noah says, pulling me back to make sure he meets my eyes as I nod. "Knox will open a portal every night around eleven p.m. for you to come here. Time works differently here now; Knox managed to slow it down. So an hour here is about three minutes back there. You could spend some more time here before you go back, if you want." I'm happily relieved to hear Knox has slowed time down. I didn't know how I was going to explain my absence when I got back.

"No, I can't. I have a guard who's gone to get me food. We have been here a good three hours now, and I can't risk that he will come back and find us gone. Not if I need to keep a pretence up," I admit. I was worried what would happen when Warren came back to find us all gone.

"I'm worried about you being around Quin more than anyone. You loved him. Hell, I treated him like a brother, and so did Sin...he can't be trusted now," Noah says. "You know that, right?"

"I hate him for what he did. Don't worry, he won't get close," I tell him. "But I want to know what happened to him. Quinton wasn't always like this, and if I can get him to help me take down his uncle, then maybe—"

"Hate and love are just one coin flip away. It's okay to hate that you love him, Sleepy, but to forgive him? That is an entirely different thing," Noah says, and I lean up, pushing his words out of my mind as I gently kiss Noah. I can't think about Quin right now, it hurts too much. Almost as much as it hurts to even think of Sin at all. I don't have to say anything as I lean back, because Noah always could read me.

"I miss him too. So fucking much," Noah admits to me and slowly wipes a tear away that fell down my cheek without me noticing it.

"I saw him," I admit to Noah.

"What do you mean?" he asks.

"I don't know how to explain it, but I'm sure I saw his ghost and had a conversation with him," I say. "Maybe I have the power to see the dead or something?"

"As far as I know, you shouldn't have that ability, Sleepy. I will ask around, a lot of the people here worked in the tales' library and history department. They might know," he says. "But be careful. It could be a dark tale messing about with you. Trying to break you."

"I would ask Lane, but they took all our books from us. I miss him," I say.

"The books have their own magic, lost and powerful magic. If you can find them and bring them here, that would be helpful too," he suggests, and I remind myself to remember to try and find them.

"That can be my job," Tavvy says, coming to

my side and looking at us both. "Sorry, I was totally eavesdropping. This room echoes."

"It's cool. Are you ready to go?" Noah asks us. I step away from him and nod once. It's going to be hard to leave here, especially as Knox is sleeping, Tobias is missing, and Noah is struggling to rein in his parents and look after everyone while grieving himself. Tomorrow night, I will be back and have more time with him. I think we both know that.

"Wait, how are we getting back without Knox?" I ask Noah.

"Knox pushed his power into this necklace. I would give you it, but there is only one, and it only works if you open the portal this side of the dimension," Noah says before pulling the necklace off and showing me the gemstone that glows red. He holds it out into the air before whispering *tales* under his breath. The gemstone projects a portal into the room, and Tavvy doesn't wait before jumping through it to the other side as Noah lowers his hand. I walk to Noah, placing my hand on his cheek briefly before stepping through the portal into our bedroom. Seconds later, the portal closes and the door to our room is knocked before it is pushed open by a dark tale in a hood, pushing a trolley of food. Warren stands like a statue outside the door, and he surprises me by pushing his hood back so I get just a small flash of bright grey eyes and white hair for a moment. It's his eyes though that worry me the most...he knows something is up. I can feel it, especially as he searches the room with just one look.

Let's hope he doesn't figure out exactly what it is anytime soon.

Chapter 6

"*H*istory of the importance," Tavvy reads out the class schedule, and it looks like we have history class all day today, except for an hour dinner break. The rest of the week looks the same, one class a day. Monday is the science of deadly poisons to use in battle. Tuesday is history, Wednesday is fighting class, Thursday is social studies and Friday is a weakness of the tales. Overall, these classes don't seem like the best time for anyone here. Someone knocks on our door before it's opened by Warren. Today, his hood is on again, and I can't see any of his features like I barely glimpsed last night. I found myself briefly thinking about him last night, wondering why he is different from the rest of the tales here except for Quin and Rueben who seem to have their own set of rules.

"Class starts in ten minutes. I am positive your new teacher does not appreciate lateness," he tells us. I'm somewhat grateful for the advice.

"Got it, thanks for the tip," I say, picking up my black cloak and wrapping it around my shoulders before clipping it up. The cloak is heavy and thick, with gaps for me to place my arms through. I pull the hood up and smile at Warren. "See, we are matching now."

"You are not amusing, Miss Dormiens," he responds. I think I am, but hey ho.

"Oh I am, and you know it, Mr. Warren," I reply, and even though I can't see it, I know he is smiling at me. Tavvy hooks her arm through mine, snapping me out of it and making me remember who exactly I'm dealing with. She looks at me like I'm crazy as we walk out the room, following Warren down the corridor.

"How can you stand to be anywhere near them? That urge to kill them is so overwhelming that I can just about talk to them through gritted teeth," she whispers to me.

"I don't feel that," I tell her, shrugging a shoulder and glancing back at Warren for a brief moment, catching a glimmer of his silver eyes under his hood.

"You're very odd and playing with fire," she says, and I look back to where we are walking.

"I don't know what you're talking about," I respond.

"Sure you don't," she replies with a small smile I don't get. We walk silently down the corridor, which is eerily quiet as we must have left much earlier than anyone else for class. I almost trip on my feet when I get a look at the new entrance hall to the academy and how much it has changed. Instead of the old, almost comfy feel to the academy, everything is now modern, mostly black and very creepy. The walls are painted black, with white lights littering the tops of the walls. The chandelier has gone, and in its place is a long flag with the symbol of the dark tales on it in silver. The bannisters of the stairs are painted silver, with the rest of it changed to look like black glass. Overall, I don't like it, but I'm sure the dark tales do.

"Seems someone went too far with good old black paint," Tavvy comments, and it makes me smile as we walk down the steps.

"Where is history now?" I turn back to ask Warren, but it isn't he who answers first.

"This way. Let me walk you there," Quin says just before he walks around the stairs. As usual, he has a long black cloak on, clipped around his shoulders. His black shirt is tight, fitting him well, and I can see he has been working out more than before. Oddly, it just doesn't do anything to me anymore. I'm starting to realise that whatever Quinton and I had is long lost, maybe even before Sin died. Though that raw pain is still so over-whelming every time I see him. "You never intro-duced me to your friend."

"This is Octavia," I tightly say.

"As long as you don't keep being an asshole, you can call me Tavvy," she says through gritted teeth, and I sense she is trying to be nice. Almost. There is too much sarcasm to say it was overall a nice comment.

"We should be getting the girls to class, Mr. Frostan," Warren interrupts with a stern voice.

"Right," Quin says and places his hands behind his back in a similar motion to how his uncle stands, before leading the way to class. I don't feel like I know this Quin at all; he is long lost from the boy I fell in love with. I think he has been brainwashed by his crackers uncle, and I'm not sure there is any coming back from that. We walk silently to the classroom, where Quin stops outside and pushes the door open after knocking once.

"Have a good class. I hoped we could hang out later after the day is done?" Quin asks. I don't want to lead him on, but some part of me knows I need to keep him as a friend to stay safe in this place now.

"Sounds good," I say, and he smiles widely before walking away. Tavvy heads into the classroom, and I go to follow her, but a hand grabs my arm. I look at the pale, large hand gently holding my arm and up to Warren's eyes which are all I can see under his hood.

"You are playing a dangerous game, leading Mr. Frostan on. Be careful, Miss Dormiens," Warren warns, but I honestly don't have a clue why he is giving me advice at all. My arm feels warm under his grip, and I look down to see his pale hand on mine, with a silver ring bearing a gold R in the middle of a circle on his middle finger.

"What do you care, Warren?" I ask, tugging my arm away and shaking my head at him.

"You're just another slave to whatever your king asks you to do. Even if your king is a murderous bastard and you know he's fucking crazy."

"If I really was a slave, I'd tell everyone about how you had a portal open in your room last night," he pauses, leaning closer as I'm paused in shock for a second. My heart beats faster, knowing he has something over me now. "Was it a fun visit from the Tale brothers, Miss Dormiens?"

"Whose side are you on?" I quietly ask, and we both stay silent as two dark tale guards walk past.

"You'll have to figure that one out on your own," he tells me and lets my arm go. I walk into the classroom, wondering if maybe the dark tales aren't as dark as we have been led to believe.

Or quite possibly Warren isn't like the others.

Chapter 7

I scream as a cat flings itself at me, swiping its claws across my face the second I step into the room. I call my powers as I grab it, holding it away from me as it desperately tries to claw me to death, looking like it has rabies or some shit. I sprinkle the dust into its face, and it falls asleep instantly. I gently put it on the floor and look over as a woman steps into the room. Her grey hair is swept up into a bun, her eyes are fully black and match her cloak, but the look of horror on her face as she sees the cat makes me step away.

"My fur baby!" she screams, running over and picking up the passed out cat. "You monster, how could you do that to an innocent creature?" she asks as I rub the claw marks on my shoulder and chin.

"Innocent? The cat attacked me, so I put her to sleep. I hardly hurt her, I'm not a monster," I reply, though I might have used more sleep dust than necessary. I do not like cats, and they do not like me. I thought I was safe at this place, but clearly not. That cat just reminds me of all the times I've been literally chased down streets by cat gangs. Yes, they have gangs, I know it.

I start to explain again, "Sleep isn't going to hurt her, Miss—"

"Miss Porter, now go and sit down this instant, you horrid students," she snaps, and her eyes change to resemble cat eyes in an instant, and when I see her hands, long claws are coming out of them. I quickly walk to a desk with Tavvy and sit down, knowing Miss Porter and I are not going to be the best of friends. Watching as Miss Porter walks away, I see a tail on her back, mainly hidden by her cloak. I watch as she carefully places the cat on the desk before stroking her lovingly.

"Cats really don't like you, do they?" Tavvy asks with a chuckle, and I can see she is trying not to laugh out loud at me.

"They never did," Sin's voice is a shock to me, and I jump out of my skin before looking to my left where the ghost version of Sin is sitting on the desk.

"Madi, you okay?" Tavvy's worried voice doesn't make me look away from Sin, who smiles at me.

"Remember that one time we got chased down three streets by four angry cats? What were we, eight at the time?" Sin asks me. I'm so shocked that I can't help but gape at him for a moment before I remember to answer him.

"Seven, and there were five cats," I reply, lifting a hand to touch him, but he shakes his head.

"Madi, you are really freaking me out now. Who are you talking to?" Tavvy asks, grabbing my shoulder and gently shaking me. I look to her for just a second, and when I look back, Sin is gone.

"No!" I whisper, placing my hand on the desk where he just was, and it's just cold. It's just a desk, and Sin is gone. My heart hurts once again, and I hear a raven squawk in the distance, but I can't see it.

"Madi?" Tavvy asks again, this time she is

more panicked than before, and it makes me take a deep breath before looking at her.

"It was Sin. His ghost, his soul...I don't actually have a clue what it was," I whisper. "But he was here."

"Sin is dead, babe. He's gone," Tavvy gently tells me, and I see she is super concerned for me. I don't blame her; I'm telling her I just saw a dead person sitting on the desk, talking to me.

"I know that, but I swear he was just here," I tell her. "You don't have to believe me, but I know it was him. He has something to do with the ravens. They are always near when he is."

"Grief does funny things to us all, I guess, but I trust you. If you say he was here, then he was. I'm just a little freaked out since I watched a ghost hunting show years ago and couldn't sleep for weeks," Tavvy says and strokes my arm before lowering her hand as the room starts filling with students. I don't know why it doesn't scare me like it does Tavvy. I guess it's because I'm so desperate to see Sin that I don't care how it happens. I just need to see him.

I look up as Ella walks into the room, looking far more like herself. Her red hair is up in a bun, and her cloak has been restyled by tying a belt around it tightly at her waist. A long slit runs from her neck all the way down, revealing her long legs in red high heels.

"That is not proper clothing attire, young lady," Miss Porter says.

"I'm no lady, Miss whatever your name is. If you want my fashion advice, I would be happy to help you," she says, placing her hands on her hips as she eyes Miss Porter's outfit.

"Just sit down. Now!" she shouts, and Ella smiles as she passes her and comes to sit at my side before winking at me.

"Welcome, students, to your new class, History of the importance. The importance in the title is the joint history we both share: the triple goddesses who created everything around us. Now we are going to be heavily studying every bit of information we can find out about them in the books in the cupboard at the back of the class. You are expected to read the books and write notes on what you find. One book a day must be completed, or you are not permitted to leave the classroom until it is done at the end of the day," she says. "And I will be checking the facts, so do not try to cheat."

"What happens if we decide to do nothing

and just leave?" Ella asks, and to be honest, I'm curious about the same thing.

"You will be sent to King Rueben for punishment. I am very good at controlling my urge to kill you all like my genes beg me to do. King Rueben is not, and you, Ella, are the child of the old Masters. It would not be a quick death for someone like you. Now get on with your work, and no talking," she demands, and we aren't left with much else but agreeing to do what she asks. None of us want to deal with Rueben on our own just yet. We need a plan, a damn good one, if we are going to stand any chance.

I slide out of my chair first, and everyone follows me to the back where I open the cupboard to find boxes of books. I open the nearest box and pull out a book, seeing that these are the old ones from the library. It makes me think of the dagger hidden in my room. This lesson makes me wonder why Rueben wants us to spend so long reading these books and what exactly he is looking for.

Chapter 8

"*Y*ou look tired," Quin comments after we have walked in silence for a good ten minutes around the academy. My feet crunch against the cold grass with every step, and snow lightly falls around us. His powers and…well, it is everything about him that I don't like. It's a stark reminder of who he is now. Whereas I used to feel comfortable in his presence, I only feel nervous and annoyed now. I want to hit him again and hope that it knocks some sense into his head and he realises how much of an idiot he has been to follow his insane uncle. Another part of me still loves him, but it's not the same love it was. It's not even a quarter of it anymore because I don't respect Quinton after what he did. Or didn't do, I guess. Respect and love have to be equal…and so does trust. I could never trust Quinton again.

"What are you a descendant of?" I ask him.

"The Snow Queen," he tells me. "Did you ever read that fairy tale?"

"No, but then I never did look at many fairy tales until I came here, and now I wish I had read them all instead of being a tomboy and playing outside all day with you and the brothers," I reply, and he chuckles a little. For just a second, it feels like us before I left. Before everything went so wrong.

"What happened after I left, Quin?" I ask him, because we can't pretend it is the same as it was back then. I want answers, and I want to know how he got to this.

"You remember how I wanted to tell you something, the last phone call we had before you went?" he asks, and I nod because I do remember. I spot a bench pressed against the stone wall, so I head over to it and sit down. Quin sits next to me, looking down at the frosty grass.

"I was going to tell you that my uncle turned up on my door and paid my mum to give him custody of me. So he moved me into the local hotel, and he started telling me everything. I was shocked at first, but then he told me where you had gone...and that I'd get powers soon if I was strong," he explains. It makes me wonder what would have happened to Quinton if he didn't get powers. I doubt Rueben would be even a tiny bit interested in him then.

"Where is your father?" I ask.

"Dead. The Tale Masters killed him not long after I was born. My uncle told me so," he says, and I get a sneaky feeling he really trusts his uncle.

"Then why didn't he come for you sooner?" I ask.

"You ask a lot of questions," Quinton replies.

"Only the ones you are trying to avoid asking yourself, Quin," I answer.

"I hate how you do that," he mutters, finally looking at me.

"Do what exactly?" I ask.

"Get into my head and confuse me. You've always been able to do it to me. It's why I love you," he says and gently places his hand over mine. I pull my hand away and quickly stand up off the bench. "I still love you." His words almost echo around me, like they are there to haunt me.

"Quin, you have no idea what love is then! If you loved me, if you knew me well enough, then you would have never let Sin die! I would have died for him; I would rather have died with him than let him die alone!" I shout at Quinton, and I can't look at him for more than a second.

"Madi, I just—"

"Couldn't let me die? Well, is this reality any better? I will mourn Sin for the rest of my life, and every time I look at you, I only see him dying. That is it for us, do you understand that?" I ask. "You don't love me, not real love, and maybe one day you will love someone enough to understand what I'm feeling right now."

"Did you ever love me?" he asks.

"That is the sad thing. I loved you as much as I loved him at one point. Or at least I thought I did. The truth is simple… I could walk away from you and move on. I could *never* do that with him. Even in death, my soul partly belongs to Oisin," I say, and he nods, looking down at the ground as I do the best thing for us both, I walk away. I head straight around the corner, bumping head first into Warren who catches me with one arm around my waist.

"Hey," I say, clearing my throat and pushing a

hand into his chest to back myself away. "I'm sorry, I wasn't looking where I was going."

"You should be more careful," he says, his voice husky, and I take a big risk by lifting my hand and going to push his cloak hood down. "Don't. You won't like what you see, Miss Dormiens."

"I'm sorry, that was rude of me," I say, letting my hand drop, and I walk around him towards the entrance to the academy without saying another word as he follows me. I only look back at him when I'm outside my room, and I'm super curious about what he is a descendant of. Everything about Warren makes me curious. Thank god I'm not a cat, or I'd have to worry about getting myself killed.

"What are you descended from? I know it's rude to ask, but I want to know," I ask him, and he doesn't reply to me as I stare at his dark hood. I shake my head, wondering what the hell I'm doing as I turn the handle of my door and let myself back into my room. Just as I close the door, keeping my eyes on Warren, he tells me the answer.

"Rumpelstiltskin."

Chapter 9

I quickly shut the door, wondering why I'm suddenly a little frightened of Warren. I vaguely remember the Rumpelstiltskin fairy tale, but I'm sure my memory is a little rusty. Something about making a deal with a girl so she can make gold or something. There was something about a firstborn child being stolen. Damn, I really need to find a human fairy tale book or a charger for my phone so I can google it.

"Hey, what did ice dude want?" Tavvy asks as I turn around to face her.

"The usual. I don't really want to talk about it," I say, and I know she understands as she comes closer and places her hand on my arm for a moment before stepping away and going back to her spot on the floor where she was reading a book. "Do you know anything about the Rumpelstiltskin fairy tale?"

"Why?" she asks, her face going a slight bit pale. I walk across the room and sit next to her as she places her book down.

"Just curious," I lie, and I have no idea why I automatically just did that.

"The Rumpelstiltskin fairy tale is one of the most famous in our world, Madi. The history books all talk about their dark line and how you should never trust a word that leaves their lips. They used to be the royals of the dark tales, the most powerful and trickiest from their very birth. Well, that is until one of them gave up the throne to the Frostans. We never knew why, only that it happened right before the peace agreement was meant to be made between the good tales and dark tales," Tavvy explains to me. "Then the Frostans declared war, and here we are today because of that war."

"Why would they give up the throne?" I ask because that doesn't make one bit of sense.

"Who knows?" Tavvy replies. "I never read an answer or heard one."

"What do you think their power is? I don't

remember a whole lot about the fairy tale, to be honest," I admit.

"Humans never got close to the truth with them, like a lot of tales, in all fairness. I didn't read the section on their powers, but they were the royals. The most powerful for a reason," she explains to me. It means I need to be more cautious around Warren, even if part of me trusts him for some insane reason. I mean, he has kept my secret about the portal, and I can't see any other reason why he would do that other than the fact he isn't on Rueben's side. I highly doubt Rueben didn't use underhanded tactics to get the throne from Warren's family, so I'm sure Warren doesn't trust or respect him. From my talk with Quinton, I'm realising Rueben is a sweet talker and very good at manipulating people. He knew Quinton craved a father figure in his life, so he used that desire to manipulate Quinton to his side. I know Quinton isn't that stupid though, and hopefully he will start to see through the cracks.

"Thanks anyway," I eventually reply to Tavvy, realising that she is staring at me, trying to understand what I'm feeling.

"Are you okay?" she asks, and I really don't

blame her for questioning me. I feel like I'm slowly losing my mind.

"Define 'okay'?" I ask her with a humourless chuckle that she sadly smiles at. I jump when there is a tapping at the window. We both quickly get up and see a raven sat at the window, tapping its head against the glass repeatedly.

"Why are the ravens so obsessed with you?" Tavvy asks. "It isn't your power."

"I don't know," I reply, watching as the raven taps and taps on the window. Before either of us can comment on the raven, a portal burns into the room, and a hand reaches out. I run to the portal, sliding my hand into the waiting one and holding my other hand out for Tavvy who grabs it. I'm pulled through the portal, straight into Knox's arms, and I stare up at him as I let go of Tavvy's hand while the portal disappears behind us. I smile widely at him because he looks better. At least more normal than the last time I saw him. His hair is brushed out of his face, he has shaved, and he smells a lot better now. His eyes still hold the same grief and pain though, even if he is trying to function.

"Right, this is awkward for me once again. Nice to see you, Knox," Tavvy says, and I can't help but smile at her words with Knox for a second as we hear her walk away.

"I'm so sorry about yesterday. I was out of order, and I—" Knox tells me, and I lift my hand, placing a finger in front of his lips.

"Don't be. You are grieving, we all are," I tell him, and he gently presses a kiss to my finger before I lower it. "There is nothing to forgive."

"I hate to ask anything of you, especially when I really want to throw you over my shoulder, take you to my room, and lock you in there so you don't go back to that academy...but I need your help with Tobias," he says, looking away from me to the woods in the distance before meeting my eyes again. "I can't lose another brother, and Tobias...well, you need to see to understand. We are having a funeral, burning Oisin's body and saying goodbye. It's important he comes tonight. We all need him there, and he needs to say goodbye."

"Where is he?" I ask, knowing it must be bad if Knox is worried about him. Knox waves a hand, creating a shimmering silver portal that looks like water. It hurts to think of a funeral...it seems so set in stone that way. I've seen Sin twice now since he died, and I don't think I'm ready to stop seeing him yet.

"I will try to help," I tell Knox.

"Be careful. Tobias isn't himself. When you want to come back or if you need me at all, just shout my name. I will be listening," he says, letting me go after pressing a kiss to my cheek. I turn back to him and wrap my arms around his waist, holding him tightly, and he holds me back, resting his head on top of my head for just a second. I step away, knowing he wants me to stay, but Tobias is more important at this moment. I need to see Tobias, to see he is okay myself. I know there is a good chance he isn't; Tobias has never taken dark emotions all that well.

I step through the portal, which is soft as it floats over me like a blanket of silk, and then I'm stood in the middle of the forest. There are large rocks all around the clearing I'm in, and those are surrounded by the large trees. My feet are in a stream, the water quickly soaking my trainers and the bottom of my leggings, though it isn't cold. The light beams down into this place, casting thick shadows over the rocks and against the stream of water travelling over the little stones.

I turn around, and that's when I see Tobias for

the first time since Oisin died. He is sitting in the stream, his head in his hands as he is hunched over, watching the water. His shirt is gone, showing off his muscular back that is tight and strained, much like how he feels to me. His skin is pale though, and there are scratches and cuts all over him, some deep and some will heal soon. I can see bits of broken rock that are still in his skin, and it's clear he hasn't bothered to look after himself.

"Tobias," I gently say his name, but he either doesn't hear me or he ignores me altogether. I carefully walk over to him and around him, but he keeps his head hidden from me. I unclick my cloak before chucking it onto the bank of the stream. I slowly sit down in the water, trying to ignore how cold it is as it soaks my leggings, and the little stones feel like they are going to leave permanent imprints in my ass. None of it matters though, not as I place my hands on Tobias's arms, and he is shaking.

"The last thing Sin said to me was that I needed to be a man and be enough for you because, right then, I wasn't. He was right, I was a fucking mess. I should have been there for my brothers and you, and because I wasn't, Sin died," Tobias says, his voice cracking like he has been screaming or shouting for days. He might have been for all I know.

"No," I say, shaking my head, even though he can't see it as he stays in the same position. "Sin died because of Rueben Frostan, and that is it. As much as I wish to any god we could change that fact...we can't."

"Then can you tell me how to live with it? I just don't know how, Sleepy," Tobias says, and this time, he lifts his head and meets my eyes. My breath hitches when I see how bad Tobias really looks. His brown hair is wet, sticking to his forehead, and it is super long now. I'd almost like his hair like this if it weren't for the fact that he has clearly given up. His brown eyes are still so beautiful with those silver specks of light in them, but they are even darker now, changed by the pain that is coming off him in waves. Pain and guilt are swallowing him whole, and I won't let that happen; I won't let him be lost because of it. Sin wouldn't want that, I know it deep inside of my heart. Tobias Tale can't be lost, because I need him. I want him, and I...love him. I always have, even though he is a hot mess most of the time now. He needs a reason to live, to fight for, and I have to hope I'm enough now.

I move closer, lifting my wet hands to his pale cheeks and lifting his head just an inch. My heart beats so loudly, almost echoing, with how nervous I am as I press my lips to his cold ones. I don't let go as his clear instinct is to push me away, to fight me off, because letting me get close to him is too risky. He is too scared of losing me. I understand that emotion perfectly and way more than I'd like to.

I'm not living for the past anymore...I'm fighting for the future. Tobias needs to do this too, or he will stay here and let the past destroy him. Tobias snaps, tugging me closer with his hands that go to my waist as he kisses me back, pouring all the pain and emotion he is feeling into a dangerous, addictive kiss. I wrap my legs around his waist, as I slide my hands into his thick, wet hair and grip his hair tightly as he deepens the kiss.

"Tobias, no more pushing me away and fighting me. I love you, and I'm going to fight for us. Please tell me I'm not fighting for nothing," I whisper against his lips. "Please." My words are nothing short of a desperate plea, because I can't lose Tobias.

"I love you too. I am never going to let you down, not anymore. Losing Sin, it made me realise life is so fleeting, and it can be gone in an instant, even for the good ones. It should have been me that died; I was the one that used drugs, got fucked up, and let you down. Sin was the good guy, the one who never did anything wrong, and yet he still lost his life. I miss my brother so fucking much, but I'm going to make him proud. I'm going to be the man he wanted me to be," he tells me, and I hug him tightly, placing my head on his shoulder. That's when I see Sin, standing in the river though it flows through him, and he smiles widely at me before disappearing. My heart breaks a little more, even though I know this is what Sin wanted for me. For Tobias.

He should be here to live with us, to hug his brother.

I will never stop loving Sin and wishing he was here...but I have to find a way to live. Just like Tobias has.

Chapter 10

I hold Knox's and Noah's hands while we watch the pillar of wood holding Sin's body as it lights on fire. The fire rapidly spreads all over the wood, spitting sparks into the air. There is almost no sound, nothing but the crackling of the fire and the beating of my own heart. The sound of my tears dropping onto the ground is a small sound as well, I guess. The smell of the fire makes me want to run away, to deny this is all happening. Tobias stands at Noah's side, and I feel all their pain like it is my own as I stand here. There are twelve other pillars floating in the big lake we are standing on the edge of, each one has a body they were able to save. Mothers, fathers, lovers and even one child. The dark tales didn't care who they killed; they just took what they wanted.

Eventually, some of the mourners break down. The cries and sobs of the people are so hard to stand here and take in. I can't say goodbye to Sin. Not yet. I let go of the brothers' hands and turn around, walking into the forest. I don't know if they are following me. I don't know anything as tears blur my vision while I walk along the pathway. I keep walking and walking until I stop right in front of Knox's cabin. I look to the pool, and before I think about it, I start taking off my shoes. I pull my black dress over my head and jump headfirst into the pool, the warm water soothing me almost instantly. I don't know how long I endlessly swim lengths up and down the pool before I relax back against the rocks, just watching the still water.

"Can I join you?" Knox's voice should shock me, but it doesn't. I nod, before pulling my eyes up to meet his as he tugs his shirt off. Knox leaves his boxers on after taking his trousers and shoes off, then jumps into the pool.

"I'm sorry I just left like that. I'm not—and I don't think I ever will be—ready to say goodbye," I admit to Knox when he stops right in front of me. I wrap my arms around his shoulders, pulling myself closer to him.

"Sleepy, I don't expect anything from you. I never have done, and I never will do," he tells me. "I just want you here. Next to me."

"I miss him," I lightly admit to Knox. I don't want to add my emotions to his bucket of them, but I just have to say it one time.

"So do I. Every moment, I feel like a chunk of me is missing, and you know the only thing that makes it a little easier?" he replies to me. I'm glad he is trying to help me and be here for me. I shouldn't have run from Knox, not him. Not Tobias or Noah either. They are my home, and they are what makes me feel better. They aren't the bad guys here.

"What?" I ask.

"Being around you. Even when I'm angry and scared, you make me feel better. I live to see your smile, to hear your laugh, and just to be next to you, Sleepy," he says. I lean closer and kiss him softly, gently enjoying his lips for a moment.

"What do you plan for our future, Knox?" I ask, because I don't want to talk about the past anymore. I haven't thought of a future since I was told it might not be in my control. I know I wouldn't have ever married Roger like the Masters planned, and I wouldn't have ever left the Tale brothers' lives. I guess I secretly hoped the Masters would change their minds, and we could live out our days together, happily. Now I don't know what I want exactly. There are three people I know I want in my life though. Three people I love and cannot live without.

"We kill Rueben for what he did. I made a vow to kill him with Noah and Tobias. Then we are going to end the war," Knox starts to explain to me, and that isn't surprising. Knox, Tobias and Noah are honourable. They couldn't relax or rest without knowing Rueben has paid and everyone is safe.

"Then what?" I ask.

"We want to take you away, somewhere with a beach, and spend a few months just relaxing. Then we could travel—I know you always wanted to see the world—before buying a little house somewhere in the tales community and living in peace," he explains to me. I wasn't expecting such a well thought out plan.

"So you don't want to live with the humans?" I ask. I've never even considered living in the tales community, if I'm honest.

"No, well, I don't want to lie to our children about who they are," Knox explains, and it makes me smile.

"Our children? Like more than one?" I ask with wide eyes. Knox is a big guy, and I can't help but imagine his children will be big babies. I'm not sure I'm ready—or ever will be—to push out a baby that size.

"I would like more than one, yes," Knox says with a big grin that makes me chuckle even if my inner thoughts worry about big babies.

"Seems you have it all planned out, Mr. Tale," I say, running my fingers through his hair. "Funny enough, I really like your plan."

"I know it's odd to have this kind of relationship in the human world, but you are okay with us all loving you, right?" he asks me. I guess they never have directly asked me if I'm okay with all of this. It's not like we planned this, but I couldn't imagine a life with them any other way than this.

"You love me, Knox?" I ask him with a silly smile on my lips.

"Yeah, Sleepy. I love you," he softly tells me. I kiss him harder this time, wrapping my legs around his waist, and he turns us around in the water so we are floating as we kiss. I eventually break away from the kiss just so I can tell him something.

"I love you too, Knox Tale," I admit and kiss him once more. "Of course I'm happy with having you all love me. I've never known anything different. Even when we were all apart, I still ached for you all. There wasn't a day I didn't think of you."

We might not have the best past, but we can plan a future that is worth living for.

Chapter 11

I tightly smile at Quin, who sits across from Tavvy, Ella and me at breakfast this morning. The black curtains are closed, so I can't see which teacher is behind them in the cage, and I hate that we have to all sit and eat here when someone is in pain. I know there is nothing we can do to help them though.

This is the first morning we have been allowed to have breakfast down here with everyone else. Warren explained that Rueben didn't want us conversing with everyone else until I had calmed down. I don't know what he is smoking to make him think I just need to calm down to get over everything that happened. I need to kill Rueben; that would sure make me feel better.

"So, Quinton, can you make it stop snowing in here?" Tavvy asks with a sigh. "Even with these black cloaks on, which by the way are bloody heavy, it's too cold for my liking."

"As you wish, Octavia," he responds, a small smirk on his lips.

"I like to be called Tavvy," she replies. "I told you that."

"Sure, Octavia," Quinton replies, and it makes me smile to see Tavvy looking ever so annoyed.

"Prince of darkness, why don't you find another table and someone else to annoy?" Ella asks, crossing her arms after dropping her fork on the plate, making it clang loudly.

"I have to go anyway. I sat with you to warn you that fighting class won't be like it was before. My uncle only lets the strong survive, and the weak will fall. You need to fight and kill if you have to," Quinton tells me. "He made me kill enough to prove my worth. If he made me do that, he will be worse on you guys. Just do it and try to forget their faces." I notice he hasn't even touched any of his food, and I have no clue why I care about that. *He is evil. Remember that, Madilynn.*

"*Some* of us don't think killing is the best way

to do things, Quin," I remark, leaning back in my seat and crossing my arms.

"Can we talk later?" he frustratedly asks me. "Alone." He makes a point to look both at Ella and Tavvy before back to me. They usually stay around to make sure I'm not alone with him, because I don't want to be. Anyways, Warren is never far away. Always watching, that one. My professional stalker who seems pissed at me, and I don't even know what he looks like. It's the definition of messed up.

"No, I made it clear I don't think we can be friends," I answer, and he shakes his head, before getting up and walking away. It's not until he is out of sight that I feel like I can breathe again. Every time I see him, I can't help but think back to our past. The long nights we spent together, all the kisses when we both were mourning the disappearance of our friends. We had each other, and in some ways, it clouded us, because I don't think either of us knew what we wanted in life. Or how to really fall in love. I loved Quin...but I'm starting to realise it's not the right kind of love that makes a relationship worth fighting for. I loved Quin like he was family, and he was safe to love because I knew he wouldn't hurt me. I've realised that being hurt is normal when you are fighting for love, and being safe just isn't. No wonder my dad always said Quin wasn't the right man for me. He knew it and I was heartbroken. I thought me and Quin were everything, but I'm sure there is a million stories of girls who thought their first boyfriend was their soulmate. I just don't think that anymore.

"He isn't going to give up," Ella points out. "If you want, I can knee him in the balls and maybe he will start using his brain to think for him at least for a little while."

"It's okay, Ella," I say, nearly choking on a laugh. "Quin will give up when he realises we didn't have anything to fight for in the first place. I will always protect Quin like family, but we need distance because it can never be more than that for us."

"A relationship with a dark tale isn't safe, I get it," Ella agrees.

"It's not because he is a dark tale; that doesn't matter to me. I don't have that urge to kill them, and I don't think they have that urge around me. Not that they talk much anyway. The reason me and Quin wouldn't work is because I know what it is like to fall in love. Brutal, breath-taking, heartbreaking love. Quin and I never once had an ounce of that," I explain to her, and Tavvy is watching me closely.

"I want to find that one day," Tavvy answers.

"Me too," Ella says, and both Tavvy and I just look at her.

"Really, Miss I've-had-sex-with-half-the-school?" I dryly reply.

"You gotta kiss a lot of frogs to find that prince," she says and winks.

"Kiss? Sure, but fu—" Tavvy is cut off as a loud alarm blasts over the speakers, signalling the end of breakfast and time for us to get our butts to fight class. We all stand up, leaving our plates on the table like we are told to do, before following the line of students out of the dining hall and out the front door of the academy. We walk quietly across the grass, and I look over to the shadows near the castle, where I can see Warren walking in them, his hood-covered face turned towards me.

I eventually pull my eyes away from him and to the gym as we go through a side door and into the same room all our fight classes were held in. Thankfully, they haven't updated the decor in here, and it looks the same as it always has. I'm tired of seeing nothing but black and silver paint everywhere. I feel like getting a rainbow pen and colouring on the walls like a kid to make the place seem somewhat alive once again.

Ella, Tavvy and I all stop in the middle of the hall, feeling the rest of the students standing right behind us, moments before the door on the other side of the room opens. Three women walk in, one after another, and I'm instantly drawn to look at their killer heels that click against the floor. The heels are green with a metal snake wrapped around them, curling up around their calves. Each of them has on exactly the same heels, and when I lift my gaze, I can see they are triplets right away. Dark, scary ass ones. They all have dark green hair, loose and falling behind their backs. They wear dark green suit dresses that have white ties, and not one part of the suit is out of place or different from the other two. Their eyes lock onto me, or at least it looks that way as they stop a good distance away, all three of them placing their hands on their hips. After a moment, two of them are almost sucked into the middle one's body. It's freaky, and more than one person gasps.

"Welcome, Lost Time Academy students, to fight class," the woman in the middle says, placing her hands together in front of her. "You may call me Mrs. Frostan."

"You are Rueben's wife?" I blurt out.

"No, I am his sister-in-law," she replies, looking at me in disgust, like she can't believe I actually just spoke. So this is going well already. Wait, sister-in-law? She must be Quin's step-mother, though he never once mentioned this family member. I doubt she likes Quin though, considering he isn't her real son and is proof of her husband having it away with someone else. "Now, if there will be no other unimportant questions, I have a lesson to explain."

"Nope, I have no more questions," I say, placing my hands in the air for a second.

"Good," she replies, though she doesn't sound happy about it. "Fighting class is here to test you, to push you as far as you will go, or watch you break. We will be playing in this class with the rules that the ancients used to play. The weak do not deserve a place in this new world, nor will we allow interference from friends."

"I'm confused, what exactly does that mean?" I ask, crossing my arms.

"That if you die or you are seriously injured,

it is not a problem. The weak will die," she replies in a snooty tone.

"Who are we fighting against? I won't kill a classmate, and I think I can speak for the rest of the class when I say they won't either. We aren't killers," I answer her. I don't know when I became the person to speak for us all, but they are all looking to me to answer.

"You kill, or you will be killed. Never mind, I will not make you fight your friends. You will fight me," she replies. "Or a version of me that is strong against you." We all watch as shadow figures of her walk out of her body until there are at least twenty versions of Mrs. Frostan in front of us. The versions all go and sit on the benches at the side of the room, and no one really knows what to say to that. It's seriously disturbing.

"Which one of you wants to go first?" the original Mrs. Frostan asks, and I go to say I will, because putting her to sleep might be a good idea if it knocks the rest of them out, when Tavvy beats me to it.

"I will." I want to grab her and tell her no as she steps forward, but Ella gives me a look that suggests I don't. She is right; it would just make

Tavvy look weak, and she doesn't need that right now.

"Good luck! You got this," I say instead. I'm going to support my best friend, and if I have to, I will help her, but I trust Tavvy. She somehow beat Ella at every fight class before this, so I know she isn't weak.

"Everyone, go and sit down," Mrs. Frostan instructs. I walk to a bench with Ella and sit down. Roger Stalk comes over and sits next to me. He still has a slight cut on his eyebrow from the black eye that one of the Tale brothers gave him, but I don't think he cares to remember that after everything that's happened. He looks as upset as most of the students are, because everyone has lost someone out there. The tales community is all but gone, and what is left is hiding in Knox's dimension, with no plans to come back to the real world and help it.

"Hey, Madi. Hi, Ella," Roger says, and I smile tensely at him, remembering at some point we were just engaged. I chuckle when I see how he stares at Ella, and when I look her way, she is giving him a look that would scare even me into looking away.

"Roger," Ella replies and rolls her eyes before

crossing her arms. I look over at the door as it opens, and Quin walks in. He looks straight my way before seeing Tavvy in the middle as he walks to stand next to Warren, who is still as a statue next to the wall. The only thing that moves is the weird spear and the floaty grey stuff which I'm sure has an actual name. Grey energy? Grey magic? I really don't have a clue. I look back to Tavvy as she takes her cloak off, chucking it to the side and calling her powers out a moment later. All of her skin takes on a shiny, glittering green colour to it. Everything from her hair to her skin is now almost all green, and dust falls to the floor around her as she floats a little from the ground.

Mrs. Frostan doesn't pause as she holds her hands out, and two long swords slide out of her hands. The swords have heads like snakes, and the metal is dark green. Tavvy seems a little thrown by this, but she hides it well, and I'm instantly worried. Tavvy can't fight without a weapon, and no matter how good she is at magic, she can't push Mrs. Frostan away for that long. Mrs. Frostan smiles like she has already won, before running at Tavvy, who drops her head, dodging the hit and sliding around Mrs. Frostan who swirls around. Tavvy jumps for the attack, grabbing

Mrs. Frostan's shoulder, and Mrs. Frostan screams, shoving her away.

"Tavvy's glitter stuff burns if she wants it to. That's always how she beat me, by simple touch," Ella explains to me as Tavvy and Mrs. Frostan fight. I start to relax a little, hoping that Tavvy might actually have a chance as she grabs one of Mrs. Frostan's swords to pull it away, but the sword changes. The sword comes alive like a snake, wrapping itself around Tavvy's arm and yanking her to Mrs. Frostan. I scream as she slams her other sword right through Tavvy's stomach before pulling it out.

I'm out of my seat, running towards her before I know what I'm doing. All I can think of is killing Mrs. Frostan for doing this. Arms wrap around my chest, and a spear is in my face a moment later, letting me know who is holding me back. I don't get to shout at Warren as I watch in shock as Quin rips Mrs. Frostan off Tavvy and catches Tavvy before she falls to the floor. He holds her up as he uses his other hand to freeze Mrs. Frostan to the ground as she screams until she is too frozen to make a sound. Warren finally lets me go, and I run to Quin and Tavvy as he picks her fully up.

"I've frozen the wound; it will help until we can get a healer," Quin explains. Why the hell did he just save her?

"Your uncle killed all the healers, jackass," Ella says, shaking her head.

"I can heal her. Put her down on the floor, and everyone has to leave the room," Warren says, and I turn back to him.

"Why would you help my friend?" I ask him. "You're a dark tale."

"I will help her because she is your friend. Now out," he says, and I nod, looking back to Quin who is looking between Warren and me. He carefully puts Tavvy on the floor, and I watch as he pushes a strand of hair out of her eyes. We all leave the room, with Ella dragging Mrs. Frostan's frozen body out, and I'm the last to follow. I close the doors, watching as Warren stands over Tavvy, his hands on his hood. I can't do anything but close the door.

"How can he heal her, Quin?" I nervously ask, rubbing my arms.

"Why don't you ask him? You seem close," he sourly replies. I shake my head at his pathetic jealous answer and look back at the steel doors for what seems like a long time before they open, with

Warren on the other side and Tavvy stood right next to him. I wrap my arms around her, and she laughs, though it's a tired laugh.

"Thank you," I tell Warren, though I can only just see his eyes under the hood. He nods his head once, and it's enough. I owe Warren a debt for saving my friend...and I will pay it back somehow.

Chapter 12

"*I* could have just slept at the academy, Madi," Tavvy says as I sit on the edge of the bed in the Tale brothers' cabin, where she has just gotten into bed. Despite Warren healing her, she still doesn't look a hundred percent right. There is a scar where the sword went through, but other than that, she just looks pale. I think it's the blood loss, because I'm sure Warren couldn't have healed that. The best thing for Tavvy is a long rest and a good meal when she wakes up.

"No, you need a good long sleep, and I want to check in on you," I tell her.

"There is no pain where the scar is. How did he do that?" she asks, and I don't know what to tell her.

"What do you remember?" I ask.

"Nothing," she says, and I nod, patting her hand once. "Did Quinton really save me?"

"Yes. I was running to you, but Warren stopped me. It didn't matter though, because Quinton was there for you," I explain to her.

"Maybe there is some good in that guy after all," she says with a small smile.

"Maybe," I reply with a tight smile back. He still let Sin die, and I won't ever forget that. It's going to take a lot more than stopping his step-mother killing Tavvy to make me trust Quinton ever again.

I slide off the bed and go to the door, blowing out the candle in the room to make it dark before leaving. I shut the door and walk down the new corridor of bedrooms and through another door into the open plan living area, where Noah is sitting on a blanket in front of the fireplace. The fire is lit, and it's making the room warm and inviting, as if being around Noah alone weren't inviting enough. He looks back at me, his lips tilting up into a sexy smile as he holds out a hand for me to take. I kick my shoes off before going over to him and sitting down, linking our fingers together as the heat of the fire warms me up.

"How is she?" Noah asks.

"Tired and, though she won't admit it, a little bit scared. Tavvy is the strong one, but the dark tales don't play by the rules. They fight dirty, Noah," I say as it's the truth. They don't have healers because they don't believe in healing the wounded. They don't care if they accidently kill someone as they think only the weak die. In truth, even the strongest people in the world can sometimes be bested by luck or chance.

"I know they do," Noah replies. "Our parents used to send us on missions to find dark tales and kill them. We were close to getting Rueben when he got to the academy and killed Sin instead."

"That's what all your missions were? Killing people?" I ask.

"Killing dark tales, Madi. There is a difference," he replies, making sure to correct me.

"What if there isn't a difference?" I say, because at the end of the day, what is the big difference between us? We are both humans with powers, descended from fairy tales. The good comes with the bad most of the time.

"They haven't done anything good to be worth saving in a long time," he responds. "What little light they once had is long gone now."

"Quin saved Tavvy when I couldn't. Warren saved her life, and he didn't have to," I explain to him. "That was good, even though they are dark tales."

"Really?" He pauses in thought, and he really seems to consider what I'm telling him for a few moments of silence between us. Until I'd met the dark tales, I thought they were monsters too. It's what I was told and scared off from the very first day of Lost Time Academy. "Maybe you're right. I just don't know anything at the moment, Sleepy. Is the war worth winning to make what little is left of our people slaves to the Masters once again? A lot of people hated that life," he tells me, rubbing my hand with his thumb as we both silently look at each other. There are so many things to discuss about the future when this war is all over, and I really don't know who is going to win in the end.

If the dark tales rule, I doubt they will let us all live for much longer, threatening their reign. If the good tales take back the control of the island and the academy, then they rule us under their thumb anyway. We have to marry who they choose, do what they say, and never have much freedom. It worked out for my parents, and they are happy, which I'm sure some people are...but for me? It would mean I couldn't love the Tale brothers. Not loving them is like taking my heart out of my chest and slamming it into the dirt. That can't happen.

"Who is Warren?" Noah eventually asks, and I realise I haven't told him or Tobias or Knox about Warren yet. Knox and Tobias are sleeping after I made them pass out with a little dust. This time I didn't have to ask or force them to rest, because they both came to me to ask. Tobias is still struggling with both grief and withdrawal from the drugs he was addicted to. There is no moon here, so he can't get them if he wanted, but I really feel Sin's death shocked him into never wanting to take another drug. Anyways, he needed sleep, and Knox never can sleep. I really want to get him alone and find out why exactly that is. I'm sure it's got something to do with the missions Noah just told me about. That has to affect you, killing people. Even when they are called the bad guys and you've been brought up to think that way.

"Warren is my personal guard, but he isn't like the others," I explain to him.

"What is his last name?" Noah asks, looking serious now.

"I don't know, but he is alright. I promise I'm not worried about Warren," I say, and I leave out the fact he knows about this place and that I come here every night. I don't know whose side Warren is on and why he keeps helping me, but I feel like I can trust him. I just need to know more about Warren. Noah seems to know I have more to say, but he looks away to the fire before back to me.

"Wait here," Noah mysteriously says, getting up and letting my hand go. I watch as he goes to the bar in the room and pulls out some things from under the bar. When he walks back over, he is holding a bag of marshmallows and two metal sticks with plastic handles. As he sits down, he hands me one of the sticks. "Remember when we went camping that one year?"

"Yes, and I also remember how Knox woke everyone up screaming that there was a bear in his tent. There are no bears in England," I chuckle, and Noah laughs. I really love Noah's laugh.

"It was so funny," Noah replies.

"It was funnier when you guys dragged Sin on his mattress out into that river," I say, chuckling as Noah remembers.

"We all thought it would be funny to see him

wake up in the river, but we didn't expect the river level to rise and float him about a mile away before he fell in," he replies with a big smile.

"I don't think I will ever forget his face when he got back to camp in just his boxers. He was one wet, mad thirteen-year-old," I say, and it's at that moment, we both remember he is gone. Sometimes I just forget and expect him to walk through the door any second, and then it's a time like this that is a stark reminder about the truth. Sin isn't coming home, and all we have left are memories now.

"Here," Noah says, offering me a marshmallow from the packet he opens. I slide the marshmallow on the end of the stick and place it into the fire. After a second, mine catches fire, and Noah laughs as I pull it back, blowing it out.

"That fire is too hot for marshmallows. I was about to say let me," he explains and holds his marshmallow on his stick up in the air. He covers the marshmallow with his hand, which glows brightly for a moment, and then there is a perfectly toasted marshmallow on the stick.

"You have your uses, it seems," I cheekily reply, and he grins as he curls a finger at me to come closer. I put my stick down at the side before crawling closer in front of Noah. He watches me closely as I peel the marshmallow off the stick and slowly eat it.

"Thanks, that was delicious," I say, and he clears his throat, before rubbing the back of his neck with his hand. Noah's cheeks are a little red, brighter than they were from the fire a moment ago anyway.

"Want another?" he asks as I place the stick away from us with the packet of marshmallows, and I shake my head as I crawl closer to him. He lifts a hand, gently running his fingers through my hair, letting it fall onto my shoulder.

"No, I want you to kiss me, Noah," I ask, because it is all I want in this moment. I want us, I want to be reminded what it feels like to be really alive.

"Do you love me, Madi?" he asks me, moving a little closer so we are a tiny bit apart. My heart pounds in my chest as I answer him.

"Yes. I always have done, and I always will do," I say.

"I love you too," he admits and kisses me. He holds my top tightly as he pulls me closer to him, pressing my chest against his before sliding his hands under my top. His hands are warm against my skin as he deepens the kiss. I tug his shirt up, and he lets me go to slowly pull it up and off his chest. I run my hands over his muscular chest, down to the rippled six pack and to his trousers. He catches my hand, stopping me and looking at me, though I can't read his expression.

"I've never. I know all my brothers did at one point or another, but for me…well, I wanted you," he confesses to me. Even though it makes me a tiny bit jealous to know the brothers have all slept with someone else, I can focus on nothing more than how sweet it is that Noah wanted me.

"Me and Quinton—"

"I know. Or I guessed. I don't mind that. At least one of us will have a clue what we are doing," he tells me, and I'm glad he doesn't seem that bothered about it.

"Let's not overthink this," I suggest, standing up with Noah. He grins and pulls me to him, kissing me once before he takes my hand and leads me to his bedroom.

"Trust me, I've overthought this moment a million times. I don't want to think anymore; I want to know what it feels like to be with you," he tells me. My cheeks burn red as we go to his room, and he shuts the door behind him. There is one candle lit, a dim one that gives a little light into the room as I walk to the bed. I pull my top off and slide out of the rest of my clothes before looking at Noah, who is watching me. His eyes almost look brighter than a pure fire as he walks to me, kissing me harshly as he presses us back onto the bed. His body covers mine as he kisses me, groaning into my mouth when I wrap my legs around him. He rolls us over, and I lean back, undoing his trousers.

"Wait, do you have any protection?" I ask Noah, and he nods. I climb off Noah so he can reach over to his bedside unit and pull out a packet of condoms. I stroke his arm as he slides one onto himself and turns to me. We both smile at each other for a second, both us shocked that we have gotten to this point, knowing that after this we both will never be apart.

"I love you, Noah Tale," I admit as I climb over him and lean down to kiss him. His hands leisurely explore all of my body, finding what I like and what makes me moan before he very slowly inches his length inside me. I gasp when we are finally together, and he flips us over so he can take control as he thrusts in and out of me. He leans down, kissing my nipple as he speeds up. We both look at each other in this moment, where we are perfectly together, and I can't help but smile at him. This is perfect, and we both know it. It isn't just the sex, it's years of knowing you are made for someone and finally getting to be with them. Noah is mine, and I claimed him a long time ago, even if I wasn't aware I did. I gave him my heart, and as he makes love to me, I know he will treasure it forever. I will cherish this perfect moment forever, too.

Noah kisses me, exploring my mouth as he thrusts in and out of me, getting faster each time. His lips move down my jaw before brushing across my neck and to the base of my throat. He softly kisses me once more, a groan leaving his lips. Seconds later, I moan his name as I come, and then he finishes moments later. We both breathlessly smile at each other as he pulls out of me and pulls me to his side.

"Was it as good as you imagined your first time to be?" I ask, curious.

"Even better." I smile at his confession as he pulls a blanket over us and slides a hand onto my cheek, staring into my eyes. "I love you, Sleepy. I always have, and I always will."

Chapter 13

"*You have to stop this all,*" *a feminine voice whispers to me, sounding like she's right next to me, but as I turn my head to the side, I'm alone in the field outside the academy. The moon hangs high in the sky, and I stare at it for a moment, before I hear them coming. The ravens. They are never far away in my dreams. I used to be somewhat scared of them, but not anymore. Now I know they have been helping me...just in their own way. Warning me. I turn around as a flock of ravens fly right at me, only missing me by an inch. They fly around my body like a black wave before they start flying in circles around me. The voice doesn't speak again, but instead, the raven screeches fill my ears next. As I fall to my knees, holding my hands over my ears from the noise being so loud it*

hurts me, I swear the ravens sound like they are screaming sleep.

The banging of our bedroom door quickly wakes me up from my power nap, where I swear I only closed my eyes for a few moments when I lay down. Gosh, I'm tired today, and I fully plan to stay in my favourite Dorito-stained hoodie and comfy leggings all day. I want to daydream about last night with Noah. His lips on mine, our first time together, and how he told me he loved me. The way he looked at me, the way he kissed me, and so much more are something I will never forget. Last night was special and a long time coming. I climb out of bed, looking up at the top bed where Tavvy is sitting up, a book in her hand, and her eyes on the door as I pull it open. Warren is standing there, his hand wrapped around his spear at his side and his hood pulled low.

"Rueben is requesting your presence," he states.

"Hey, creepy boy, do you know where Quin is?" Tavvy asks, getting off the bed, and I look at her oddly as she pulls her shoes on.

"I saw Quinton in the dining room last," Warren answers.

"Why do you want to see him?" I ask her.

"I'm going to say thank you. I need to say it. I've already told Warren here thanks this morning, but as you saw, he didn't seem to care all that much," Tavvy says, and I chuckle, remembering how awkward it was as Tavvy rambled on about how thankful she was that Warren saved her life, and after all that, Warren simply replied, "Fine." Then he turned around and continued his guarding of our door as Tavvy shut it.

Tavvy hugs me tightly while whispering in my ear, "I'm going to tell Quin you are with his uncle. He is the only one that can come and watch to make sure Rueben doesn't hurt you." I smile as Tavvy lets go of me and walks out of the room. I let go of the door and put my shoes and cloak on before going out and walking down the corridor. I stop, looking to Warren to lead the rest of the way, and he nods his head to the stairs. Warren stays at my side as we head down the stairs and past the dining room, where I briefly look in to see who is in the cage.

Miss Noa is gone, and instead Miss Aquana is in there, beaten and looking very cold. Tavvy has her arms around Ella as she cries, and there is no sign of Quin. I can't help Ella right now, even though my heart breaks for her. I know she loved Miss Aquana, and they were very similar in some qualities. I remember seeing them hug after class once, and Ella was laughing at something she had said. We're all grieving the loss of loved ones, but it must be torture to watch them suffer this way.

"Do you think that is right?" I ask Warren as we head down the corridor. "Or do all you dark tales live off pain and death?"

"Miss Dormiens, you are quite clueless to the world, and it will be your downfall one day," Warren points out. It almost sounds like advice but wrapped in a threat nonetheless.

"Are you threatening me now, Warren?" I ask as he stops, and he turns to me.

"I threaten everyone I'm around, Miss Dormiens. Don't make the mistake of being my friend and expecting to be safe," he tells me. Now I feel like he is just trying to push me away. Warren is confusing, and I don't even know what he looks like. Or his last name. But I'm starting to realise that it's not important. Even when he hides most of himself from me and everyone else, you can't miss how different he is.

"That is the funny thing though, Warren, I feel like, for some strange reason, I am safe around you," I tell him. Warren clearly is going to say something back when the door is opened, and Rueben smiles at me. Rueben looks more like a king today, not that I will ever call him that. A king is someone whose rule you respect, and I will never respect anything Rueben has done. His black cloak has a silver lining, his white hair is styled more than usual, and his blue eyes are locked onto me.

"Miss Dormiens, I have been looking forward to this day ever since I heard of your existence," he explains to me.

"And what day is this exactly?" I ask. I don't want to know the answer that badly though. I want to go back to my room and go back to sleep.

"The day we test your true powers. Come in," he says, and I feel like I'm walking into the lions' den with no weapons. Warren might be right, the fact I really do know nothing about this world might just get me killed.

Chapter 14

"*P*lease sit down, Miss Dormiens. Would you like a cup of tea?" Rueben asks, waving a hand at the little counter on the side of the wall where there is a mini kitchen set up. "Or would you prefer to keep glaring at me and making us all feel awkward?"

"No offence, but I wouldn't trust you not to poison the tea," I reply. "And thanks to you forcing me to take poison classes, I know most poisons don't work for a long time…until they kill you." This is a total lie, considering poison class isn't until Monday, but I want to annoy him a little bit to see how far I can push him and knock him off his game.

"I dislike how people offend you and say 'no

offence' before they do. It's quite the annoying contradiction, but never mind," he remarks. "Straight to business, it seems." I move and sit down in the chair on the other side of the oak desk where Miss Ona and Miss Noa used to sit when I came in here. Now they are dead, and it's hard to accept that I couldn't help them one bit.

"What do you want?" I ask, crossing my arms and feeling more than tense about being in here alone with this psychopath.

"First off, I would like to thank you for being a good friend and later on girlfriend to my nephew. I did not know of his existence until a few weeks before I came to get him," Rueben states. I don't want him to thank me for anything, and if he thinks I can't see straight through this little game he is playing, then he is bat shit crazy.

"Did your brother not tell you about Quinton then?" I ask, because I might as well play along with this manipulation attempt.

"My brother cared only for himself and his throne. There was no place for much else, and he made it clear that children were not something he wanted. Oddly, he cared for Quinton and kept him a secret until I found out," he tells me, and he cracks his knuckles as he stares me down. I hate when people do that. So gross. I straighten up in my chair before replying to him.

"How did you find out?" I ask.

"That is a story for another day," he replies with a creepy smile.

"So it's a secret you don't want Quin knowing about," I figure out quite quickly. Quinton told me his uncle told him that the good tales killed his father. I wonder if the truth is a little bit more complicated than that.

"You are smarter than you look, aren't you, Miss Dormiens?" he asks, crossing his arms and resting back in his chair. "Even at just seventeen, you are figuring this world out far more than I expected you to be able to."

"I'm only a few months off being eighteen, and yes, I am figuring out *many* things," I say and tilt my head to the side. "Mr. Frostan, I will make sure you lose your throne before this is all over. We aren't playing on the same team here."

"We are, you are just very unaware of it yet. Maybe you aren't as intelligent as you think you are," he says, and he smiles. "Do call me Rueben. Or King Frostan. One or the other."

"Mr. Frostan, why am I here?" I ask, getting straight to the point.

"Have you heard of the raven prophecy?" he asks me, leaning back in his seat and folding his hands together.

"No," I reply, but anything concerning ravens catches my attention recently.

"I expect you wouldn't have; the good tales wouldn't want you to know of it," he replies. "See, the prophecy means you are more powerful than they are. Than their Masters."

"Me?" I ask.

"Yes, Miss Dormiens. I will tell you the prophecy because you are special, because I believe you are the only one it is meant for. The good tales planned your birth perfectly, and I bet they were more than delighted that you were blessed with any powers at all," he states, and I shift uncomfortably in my seat.

"I don't understand what you are talking about," I answer, and I hate the look he has. Like he knows so much more than I do.

"Long ago, the last of the seer line died. Every seer would have the same prophecy, but none would speak of it until the last of their blood had found their time or the prophesied one was born. The last seer could not have children due to a childhood injury, and she died naturally in her eighties. On her death bed, she told the dark and the good Masters the raven prophecy," he explains to me. "Oddly enough, your ancestor was killed the very same day, but her sister, who never received powers, carried on your bloodline and was closely watched. As was your mother's line."

"What does the prophecy say?" I ask, trying not to feel worried about this all. Secrets seem to have a nasty reason why they are secrets in this world.

"The Master only told us part of it, and only the Masters know the rest, but this is what we do know...

When the ravens come,

The ancient tales will succumb.

The raven crows, the raven knows.

When the raven dies, sleep will arise,

For sleep and war are destined for only ruin.

The raven will fall, the world will sleep.

For only a beauty can survive the deep sleep."

He stops talking, and I just repeat the words over and over in my mind. Sleep, ravens and destined for ruin? Something about a war was in there too. I don't have a clue what it means, but I have a sickly feeling in my gut that it is about me.

"You think the prophecy is about me?" I ask, but I know the answer. Of course he does. That's why I'm here and why he is so interested in me.

"Did your grandmother ever speak to you about her schooling here?" he asks, rather than answering my question, because we both know the answer.

"No, I haven't spoken to her about much since I got my powers," I tell him, still cautious because he looks way too interested in my every response.

"Your raven powers—"

"I have sleep powers. I never inherited those powers from my mother's line," I inform him to make sure he isn't getting this all wrong. I don't tell him about the dreams or the ravens that follow me around.

"You did, and we both know it. The ravens follow you, just like they do your grandmother. I believe you are the child of the prophecy, and you have both powers available to you. They could even be one," he states.

"My grandmother apparently has wings with her powers, and I do not, so you are wrong," I answer.

"Wings are a tricky thing to earn in the tales

world. You are not just given them. Did you not learn that yet?" he asks me.

"Nope, I missed a bit of school when some assholes started a war and took it over," I sarcastically reply.

"You are lucky I like you, Miss Dormiens," he sourly replies. "If anyone else spoke to me the way you do, it would be a different ending for them. Your blood defends you this time or until I am done with you." The room feels a lot colder all of a sudden, and the frost on his jacket spreads up his arms.

"I'm lucky you want something from me, Mr. Frostan," I retort. He tensely laughs and stands up, crossing his arms as he walks around the desk to me.

"In the prophecy, the second line mentions the ancient tales, do you know of them?" he asks.

"The triple goddesses that created...well, everything," I say, vaguely remembering reading somewhere that they are also called the ancient tales.

"Correct. I know that they used to live in this very academy, and I believe the two that were left spent the last of their days here before locking themselves away from the world," he explains to me.

"That's crazy. I'm sure I would have seen two goddesses lying around somewhere," I reply.

"It's not crazy. I know I'm right, and I want you to see it," he remarks, and he pulls out a smooth black stone with a white raven etched into it. "This is a raven stone, and it did belong to your grandmother."

"Did?" I ask.

"She gave my father it many years ago," he replies. "They rather loved each other, but as you know, our kind cannot be together. My father went on to marry my mother and have two sons, but he did always look out of the window like he expected your grandmother to come back into his life. She had married and had your mother and never looked back."

"That's a sad story, but why are you telling me it?" I ask.

"The raven stone used to boost her powers and let her see into the past. She gave it to my father because she never wanted to see the past again. They used to share visions; it's what the stone can do. Now I want you to look into the past, into the very beginning of the academy," he informs me, and I know he has been planning this for a long while.

"I'm not my grandmother, and I don't have her powers," I nervously answer.

"Neither of us believes that, Miss Dormiens, and I am not asking," he strictly answers.

"What happens if I say no?" I ask.

"I will kill every single good tale in this academy and make you watch," he says. His tone completely changes in a moment, and it's seriously disturbing because I know he means it. His eyes also glow blue for a moment, looking like one of those creepy White Walkers from *Game of Thrones*. I don't say another word because it's pointless, and I won't risk anyone else because of my own stubbornness. It's only a stone, and I doubt it will work anyway. I'm not the child of the prophecy; I'm not what he wants me to be. I'm just Madilynn Dormiens.

I hold my hand out, and he smiles as he steps closer. He keeps his hand on the stone as he drops it into my hand. "Go to the past. To the start of the academy. You need to focus on what you want to see."

I go to tell him nothing is happening when my hand starts to feel like it's burning. A scream leaves my lips as a white light flashes before my eyes. I focus on the academy, on the goddesses and the past like Rueben said, until the bright light is gone and I can open my eyes to see I'm in an old room. I don't recognise it, but I look to my left where Rueben is smiling at me like this is a great victory. I cry out as I fall to my knees, a burning pain slamming into my stomach. Rueben walks in front of me, clearly going to search the room as I try to see through the pain. Something isn't right.

I look up as two women come into the room. They have floor-length blonde hair, long white cloaks over long dresses made from a blue material. What strikes me the most is how stunning they are...like the very air around them even shimmers, which makes them all that more striking. They both look nearly the same, and only one thing is different about them. The woman on the left has a long scar down her cheek. I soon realise that these are the goddesses, because who else could they be? Sweat pours down my cheeks as it feels like everything is burning, everything hurts so much more than it should. I cry out, but no one hears me as I fall to the floor. I can only look up at them, blinking the sweat out of my eyes as a metal taste fills my mouth.

"Sister, are they ready yet?" the one asks.

"Soon. I am not as quick at crafting metal as I once was. The power I used to fix your mistake cost me dearly," the one without the scar replies. She stops, looking around the room, and for a brief second, her eyes stop on me before her sister talks.

"And we will fix it once more with this weapon. If we take all their powers back, we will again be as powerful as we once were," the sister replies.

"They will all die for this plan to work," the one goddess says, moving to sit on the stone basin in the centre of the room, and I scream as light flashes into my vision. When I open my eyes, I'm back in Rueben's office, in someone's arms as my legs give in. He catches me, picking me up as I look up into his hood. Warren holds me close to him as everything fades in and out. He saved me, and he is protecting me, but I don't understand why. I hear someone else come into the room, moving to stand in front of us, and the flash of white hair lets me know it's Quin before he speaks.

"I want to see more! How dare you interrupt, Warren! You are not the prince any longer, and you are bound to serve me! Not her!" Rueben shouts at us. He was a prince? And he's bound to Rueben? *Why?* I have so many questions I want to ask, but instead, I cough, splattering blood all over my hand which held the stone Rueben now holds. Warren never answers Rueben, he just looks down at me, and I can only stare back.

"Uncle, enough. Look at her. If you force her to go back again, Madi will die," Quin shouts back. "I can't let you kill her."

"No, you are right. It was a good practice run. Do take her back to her room and—" I must have blacked out, because that is the last thing I hear Rueben saying before I let the darkness take me to rest as Warren holds me close. He is my protector, my guard, and without realising it, I'm quickly wanting him around all of the time.

Chapter 15

"You can leave now. Both of you," I hear Tavvy say, sounding very nervous, as I blink my eyes open. Someone is wiping my hand with something cold, and it stings as I look up to see Warren sitting on the edge of my bed, with my hand in his as he applies a cream to my palm. He pulls out a bandage from the wrapper as he sees I'm awake, though I can only just see his eyes under his hood.

"You saved me. Why would you do that?" I ask, because I have a feeling I might have died if I kept us in that vision. I don't know how to explain it, but I'm not meant to use the power to look that far back. It was killing me.

"I don't know. I shouldn't have," he replies, and I know he means that.

"You're awake!" Tavvy happily shouts, coming over to me and offering me a hand to help me sit up next to Warren who bandages my burnt hand. "How are you feeling?"

"Sore but alive thanks to Warren," I say, feeling a little dazed as Quin comes over and takes my other hand, which I pull away on instinct.

"Sorry, I feel a bit weird. Thank you for stopping your uncle," I tell him.

"I get it, and it's okay. I'm just happy to see you awake, even though you look very pale," he replies, moving his eyes to Warren, who is finishing the bandage, before back to me. "Do you want a drink or anything?"

"I can do that. Why don't you two get out of here?" Tavvy interrupts, sounding very nervous and panicked.

"Why are you trying so desperately to get us to leave?" Quinton asks Tavvy, and it's only then that I look at the window and see it's night. The Tale brothers will be here soon, and Quinton can't know about the other dimension. Before I can ask them to leave, a portal burns into the middle of the room, and Knox steps out. There is nothing but silence for an awkward moment as Knox and Quinton look at each other. That is until Knox grabs Quin by his cloak and drags him into the portal. *Shit.*

"Y-you can't tell anyone!" Tavvy says, looking at Warren with wide eyes, but I'm not worried. It's Quin knowing that I'm more worried about—if Knox doesn't kill him first.

"Warren already knows," I tell Tavvy, who looks shocked, as I turn back to Warren. "I have to go and save him."

"I will guard the door," Warren says, slowly letting go of my hand before walking out of the door. I stand up, swaying a little bit, and Tavvy wraps an arm around my back to hold me up.

"You sure you're okay?" she asks, and I nod, walking to the portal. Just before we go through it, she whispers to me. "And we need to have a chat about what is going on between you and sexy guard man." I know we do, but right now I think we need to worry about saving Quinton. As we appear in the dimension world, Knox is on top of Quinton, beating the utter shit out of him with punch after punch. There is blood all over Quinton's face and Knox's hands and also the grass on the ground.

"Stop!" I shout, but neither of them pays any attention. Quinton doesn't fight back; he doesn't use his powers to stop Knox.

"Fight back, you bastard! You let Sin die! He was a fucking brother to you!" Knox roars at Quinton. Noah and Tobias get here just as Knox wraps his hands around Quin's neck, and I have no doubt he wants to kill him. Noah and Tobias pull Knox away, grabbing their arms around him as he struggles to get away. The world spins a little as I walk into the middle of them, and I wipe a hand across my nose.

"Madi, what happened? Are you okay?" Knox asks, snapping out of his glaring with Quin when he sees the blood on my hand from my nose. Great, bleeding again. Noah and Tobias surround me as I sway a little. The world is a little blurry.

"What happened to your hand? Madi talk to us," I'm not sure who said it as everything is hazy.

"I—" I don't get to say another word before I'm falling, and this time I don't notice who catches me as I pass out again.

"There, that should help for a short time," a female voice says, one I don't recognise. "There was internal bleeding, and whatever she did should not be done again. Her body is not immortal."

"Thank you," I hear Noah say as I open my eyes, just in time to see a purple-haired woman walk out of the cabin from where I'm lying on the sofa. I look up to see I'm on Noah's lap, and he smiles at me. Noah helps me sit up so I can see everyone is in the room, and all their eyes are on me. Knox and Tobias are leaning against the fireplace. Tavvy and Quin are sitting together on the other side, and Quin has an ice pack on his cheek. I'm sort of glad they didn't kill him. He doesn't deserve that, even if I still struggle to look at him and not see Sin dead.

"How are you?" Tavvy asks as Noah tucks me into his arm, and I pull the blanket over me as I feel cold.

"Better. Much better. Who was that?" I ask. "I didn't get to thank her."

"One of the Masters' children we got out. She is a healer, but she takes energy from other people to do it. We all gave some energy to save you," Knox gently explains to me.

"That's why everyone looks so tired," I say, and Noah nods, but not one of them looks like they regret their actions.

"Madi, what did Rueben do?" Knox gently asks me.

"I didn't know what he wanted with you or that he would hurt you. I'm sorry," Quinton tells me. I nod at him before pulling my eyes down.

"He thinks I'm the child of some raven prophecy," I answer their unspoken question.

"I've heard it, but it doesn't make sense. What is the end game? That prophecy talks about sleep and ravens and war," Tobias says, rubbing his chin.

"I know what he wants, if that helps," Quinton interrupts.

"Talk then," Knox snaps at him.

"I didn't want to give you hope before, but I'm guessing all these secrets aren't helping any of us stay alive," Quinton says, scrubbing his face.

"I don't understand," I ask, sitting up further.

"My uncle wants to awaken the two goddesses and kill them, taking their power for himself," Quinton explains. "He told me all about it and how he has a dagger that is said to kill them. With the dark tales' crown he already has, he could rule endlessly."

"I saw the goddesses. We both did. He made me take him into the past, and I saw them both for a few minutes," I tell them all, and everyone is speechless. The goddesses have always been nothing more than rumours, but they are where we all came from. To actually see them is something I know I will never forget and will always treasure.

"That's incredible, if only it didn't hurt you so badly," Tobias states.

"Warren woke me up, and if he hadn't, I think I would be dead. It's not meant to be done like that. I can feel it," I explain to them. That's why the cost was so high for me.

"I will thank this Warren when I see him next," Knox says, and I smile at him.

"I had an idea other than my uncle's plan. Despite what you may think, I did love Sin like a brother. You Tale brothers and Madi are the only family I've had and ever cared about. I just couldn't save Sin and Madi, so I chose Madi. I made that decision, and I pay the price for it every day because I lost a brother and the girl I was in love with. I came up with a plan to fix it all, but I need to be close to my uncle. When he brings the goddesses back, I'm going to save the good one that created the good tales and ask her to bring Sin back to life," he tells me, and this time, no one knows what to say. Could it work?

"Do you think she could do that?" I ask, leaning forward and staring at him for an answer.

"If his soul is still around, maybe," Quin replies. "I've been researching them as much as possible, and I know they have that power."

"It's a chance, but we are talking about bringing goddesses that are lost to the world back to life," Tavvy interrupts. "Powerful goddesses that could turn around and kill us all."

"My uncle will never stop until he finds a way. He wants to destroy the world and have dark tales rule. The dark goddesses' powers are the best way to do that. He isn't strong enough on his own," Quin explains. "I soon figured out how crazy he really is. Trust me, he won't give up. I won't either, because the only person that could help us get Sin back is a goddess. I still remember when he came to talk to me before all this."

"What? When?" I ask, and I see how Knox, Tobias and Noah all don't look at me.

"A few weeks after you moved to the academy. Did they not tell you?" Quinton asks.

"Nope. *Somehow* it didn't get mentioned," I say, raising an eyebrow at Noah who looks at me first.

"We checked in on him because of that phone call you had. Sin was the only one who actually spoke to Quin as we all figured out he had powers and not the good kind," Noah explains.

"Sin told me I could make a choice. That being a dark tale didn't mean I had to choose to follow darkness and evil. He was right, and I didn't see it until he died," Quinton admits. "I was too busy latching onto the only family member who had ever cared about me. I should have seen that I had family all along, and they were who I shouldn't have betrayed."

"You should have told me," I say to the Tale brothers, because I don't have an answer for Quin.

"I know." Knox is the one to reply, but I know he is speaking for them all. "Quin, you must go back to the academy. If my parents or any Master sees you here, they will kill you, and then our chance of getting Sin back is gone." Knox waves a hand, and a portal appears behind the sofa.

"I'm going back too. See you in a few hours,

hunny. Make sure you rest," Tavvy says, standing up with Quin. I smile at her as I wave goodbye and watch as she walks into the portal after Quin, and it disappears.

"I'm going to sleep for a bit, is that okay?" I ask Noah, Tobias and Knox. "Could you all stay close?"

"We aren't going anywhere, Sleepy," Tobias says, coming over and sitting on the floor in front of me so I can rest my hand on his shoulder, which he rests his head on. Knox doesn't say anything as he sits on the end of the sofa, lifting my feet and gently rubbing them as I lie on Noah's lap and get comfy. It's not long until I'm drifting off to sleep, praying for no more dreams. For once...sleep doesn't feel safe anymore.

Chapter 16

"I have a question," I start off, looking up at Warren still hidden under his hood as we walk back from class. Tavvy hasn't finished her reading yet and told me to go back without her. "When do you find the time to eat? I mean you are never eating at meals with me."

"I can conjure food whenever I please," he explains to me.

"Can you conjure Doritos? I miss them so much, and I'd love you forever if you did," I ask.

"What are Doritos?" he asks, and I look up at him in utter horror. The poor man has never eaten the most delicious crisps in the world...well, at least in my opinion. I go to explain them when we hear a female cry and shout, and it sounds familiar. I don't wait for Warren as I run down the corridor, swing myself around the corner, and freeze for a second at the sight of three hooded dark tale guards beating the crap out of a girl on the floor. It takes me another second to realise that girl is Ella.

"Hey, dickheads!" I shout, lifting my hands full of dust as they look at me and choose to run at me a second later. I smile as I throw dust at them, and each of them collapses to the floor a moment later.

"It seems you did not need my help after all," Warren says in a surprised tone as he steps to my side while I wipe the dust on their cloaks. I run to Ella the moment the dust is off my hands and pull her onto my lap, checking for a pulse on her neck which I find. She is covered in blood, her nose looks broken, and her lip has a deep cut in it. Warren kneels next to me and shakes his head.

"To do this to a woman is a deeply disgusting act. They should be ashamed, which I doubt they are," Warren says and places his hand over Ella's on her stomach. "I can heal her a little. Enough to make sure nothing is permanent."

"Thank you," I say, and he nods, pausing as he looks at me. "I use eternal light to heal, and it would blind anyone but my bloodline. If I was healing anything greater, I would ask you to leave the area, but right now, I need you to close your eyes, and you must not open them."

"I promise I won't. Thank you for telling me that," I say, placing my hand over his for a second, and he surprises me by turning his hand, squeezing mine gently before letting go.

"You are the only person outside my family that has ever been told one of our secrets. In my family, secrets are worth more than life," he explains to me.

"Then it is a secret I will take to my grave," I promise him.

"Not anytime soon you aren't," he is quick to reply, and I smile at him, feeling butterflies in my stomach as my cheeks burn a little red. Before I can say anything stupid, I close my eyes. Seconds later, I hear Warren whisper something I can't understand before warm light glows against my skin. It feels perfect, safe and almost kind. It makes me want to open my eyes and bask in the light, but I promised I wouldn't. I don't open my eyes until the light is all gone, and when I do, Ella has only a few bruises under the dry blood on her face.

"Thank you," I tell Warren, and he nods at me as he slides his arms underneath Ella, lifting her body as we both stand up. I look at the three passed out dark tales on the floor and back to Warren, because I'm not sure what we should do about them.

"I will come back and deal with them after we return your friend to her room," he tells me, and his disgusted, angry tone makes me shiver.

"Okay," I say, and as I walk past them, I make sure to sprinkle more sleep dust all over them so they aren't going anywhere. I lead Warren back to Ella's room, and I open it for him. Ella's room is pretty, and I've never been in it before to see how nice she keeps it. There is a big dark green fluffy rug on the floor, which matches her light green bedsheets. She has a pretty white dresser, a box with a range of stuff on it where there is only one bed in the room. It's pretty big in here too, making me think Tavvy and I lost out on room choice. Warren gently puts Ella on the bed, and I tuck her in with the blanket before walking to the door, catching Warren's arm as he tries to quickly leave.

"Hey, wait," I say, and he looks down at me. More than once, I wish I could see what he looks like underneath his hood, because I feel like I'm getting close to a stranger if I don't. "Thank you. I wanted to say thank you, you know, again."

"I'm your guard and your friends' guard if you need me to be," he tells me so formally, but I don't believe he is just doing his job with me. It's more than that.

"Why are you bound to Rueben? Will you tell me?" I softly ask.

"It's a long story for another day, but let's just say I'm alive when the rest of my family isn't, due to that bond," he explains to me.

"Your family used to be the royals of the dark tales, right?" I ask. I wish I could see his face to know if I surprised him or angered him by knowing that.

"Yes, and my father made the mistake of betraying his council, which Rueben lead. He was going to make a deal with the good tales for peace," he explains to me.

"So Rueben killed him?" I ask.

"No, his brother did, and then he took the

throne. Rueben came to kill me, but instead, he offered me a choice. I follow him, bound to protect him, or I will die. I made a promise, and here we are," he replies. "When Rueben's brother fell, he took the throne, and now I'm indebted to the king."

"So it's only words and not magic that binds you to him?" I ask.

"Words have more magic than you think, Madi," he softly replies, and my breath hitches at the tone. He has never called me anything but Miss Dormiens before, and I really like how my name sounds on his lips. Not that I know how it looks to see him say my name. Before I can say anything, he steps away from me and clears his throat. "I will deal with the dark tale guards before returning. Do stay here." I nod, rubbing my arms as I watch him hurry away. I quickly go to my room and get a bowl, a towel and a bottle of water before going back to Ella's room and shutting the door behind me. I go and sit next to Ella, pouring some water into the bowl and using the towel to gently wipe the blood off her face and neck. I'm brushing away her hair when she groggily wakes up, flinching from the pain she is no doubt in.

"W-what?" she says, rapidly looking around then relaxing when she sees she is in her room.

"Just rest, Ella. You're okay now," I tell her, and she does, resting back but staying awake. I wash the towel in the bowl of water as she watches me and slowly starts to cry.

"Ella," I gently say, placing my hand over hers. "It's okay."

"No, it's not. The world is fucked up, Madi," she says, her voice catching on a sob.

"I know it is, but you can't let it beat you, Ella. Not yet," I tell her. If the world has beaten Ella down, then there is no hope for the rest of us.

"I o-only told those guards I wouldn't fuck them. The moment I said no, they started beating me, and if you hadn't been there..." she drifts off before bursting into tears. I hold my arms around her until she calms down a little.

"They won't touch you again. Warren is going to deal with them," I say as I pull back.

"He is one of them," she says.

"No, he isn't. I trust him. Completely. Warren might be a dark tale, but he is on our side. Now rest," I tell her, and I hold her hand until she falls asleep. I'm sad that this happened to Ella, and I wish I could make it all better, but I'm selfish. I'm happily going to ask the goddess to bring Sin back to me, instead of saving the world as we know it.

Love makes you selfish because there is nothing you wouldn't do, no line you wouldn't cross, to save someone you love.

Chapter 17

"I don't think green is your colour, Madi. I would suggest blue...and maybe something brighter. Are all your tops this big and well—"

"Comfortable?" I fill in for Ella, though I doubt she was going to use that word. I don't know how she is in my room, going through my closet and telling me how awful my clothes are, but this is us now. Tavvy just smiles at me from where she is lying on the bed, after Ella just went through her wardrobe. A bored Ella is a nightmare. This is what I've learnt today. Someone knocks the door, and I'm jumping up to open it as quickly as possible. Please say Warren has come to save me.

"Can I come in?" Roger asks the second I open the door. Warren is watching from the other side of the corridor, hidden in the shadows.

"I can get rid of him if you wish, Miss Dormiens," Warren suggests in a dark voice. Roger gulps in fear as he stares at me. I smile and open the door, chuckling.

"Warren is a big softy, don't worry," I tell Roger, trying to put him at ease as well as wind Warren up. He isn't a big softy as far as I know. Mr. Serious would be a better nickname for him.

"Yeah, okay," Roger grumbles as he walks in the door before I shut it.

"What do you want?"

"I know Ella has been a bit down recently and—"

"I have been fine, thank you very much," Ella snaps, placing her hands on her hips and glaring at Roger. Roger shouldn't be scared of Warren when he has a bored Ella to deal with.

"I didn't mean to upset you. I just wanted to tell you all I heard something important, and it might cheer everyone in the academy up. Well, the good tales that is," he says, rubbing the back of his thick neck with his hand.

"What did you hear?" Tavvy asks, sitting up on the bed. I cross my arms as Roger starts to talk.

"I was staying behind after history because I couldn't read half my Latin book, but that doesn't matter. I was walking back to my room, and I hear King Frostan telling three guards that he is doing to destroy the magical descendant books tomorrow. He said they were being kept in his office," he starts to explain, but I interrupt him.

"Why is this good? I love that book. Lane will be gone," I say, rubbing my chest. Lane doesn't deserve that, and I really miss him. He was a terrible guide that got me lost and in trouble most of the time, but he belongs to my family. I know the rest of the good tales feel the same way. Those books are hope to us. They are our past and future rolled into one.

"Cherry was so sweet. I don't want to lose her," Ella says, rubbing her arms in a nervous way and looking more than upset. Cherry must have been her book, which I never knew the name of.

"No, you don't get it. We know where the books are. There are only two guards, and every day for thirty minutes, King Frostan goes for a walk with prince Quinton around the academy, which they are about to do. We could go and get the books. Madi can knock the guards out and then—"

"You are brilliant, Roger!" Ella excitedly exclaims, jumping into Roger's arms and hugging him tightly as his cheeks burn red. I look at Tavvy who winks at me. Someone has a little crush, I think.

"I love the idea. We should save them and bring them here," I suggest.

"Why here?" Roger asks, but I'm not going to tell him about the other dimension.

"I can keep them safe, I promise," I say, knowing I can put them in the other dimension tonight, and they will be alright.

"I have an even better idea. A temporary fix. I will be right back!" Ella says and walks out of the room, holding Roger's hand as she drags him along with her. I briefly speak to Warren, who reluctantly agrees to look the other way and pretend I've stayed in my room if anyone asks, before I go to Ella's room with Tavvy. We wait outside after knocking, and Ella soon opens the door.

"Let's go," she says, leading the way with Roger closing the door after her. I don't ask what she was doing the whole time as we carefully sneak our way down the corridor and down the stairs. Without running into anyone, we luckily get to the corridor which Rueben's office is on, and I call my dust. I blow it into the air, and thanks to Ella, who blows a cold breeze out of her hand, it hits both the guards in the face before they can see us. They collapse to the floor, and we run over. Roger and Tavvy grab the guards as I open the door, and they drag them in before Ella closes the door. On the desk are dozens of books. All the magic books. I don't know how I know, but I pick up the one on the edge under two others and open it up. I'm so relieved to see Lane's floaty face as he grins up at me.

"Miss Dormiens. I've missed you," Lane says, and I'm so relieved to hear his voice.

"Are you okay?" I ask him.

"I'm a book, of course I am," he responds, and I roll my eyes.

"I've missed you too, Lane," I tell him.

"Of course you did, I am an exceptional friend," he replies.

"How are we going to move all these books?" Tavvy asks as Ella pulls open a large red bag. I watch as the books are all sucked into the bag like a vacuum after she whispers a word in Latin I can't pronounce.

"What was that?" I ask in shock.

"Oh, it's an heirloom of my line, but I just use it to sneak stuff into the academy. That's why my room is so pretty," she explains to me. "Now hand your book over. We can't risk anyone seeing them here, and then you need to take the bag. I want the bag back though." Ella knows about the other dimension, but she decided to stay here so as not to arouse suspicion.

"One second," I say, and she nods, looking away. Tavvy and Roger just drop the guards in the corner, and I look down to Lane.

"Lane, do you know much about the Rumpel-stiltskin line?" I ask him.

"The Nightshade royal family line, you mean?" he asks.

"Is that their last name?" I ask.

"Yes. They are tricksters and known to have incredible powers due to their ancestor making a deal with a god. I do not know more, I'm sorry," he replies.

"It's okay. We will speak more later, okay?" I ask.

"Promise?" he asks.

"Of course," I tell him and smile as I close the book. I place the book into the bag, which vacuums it up so it looks like the bag is empty. Ella hands me the bag as we leave the office as quickly as we can. When I get back to my room, I hear Rueben shouting downstairs. Warren only shakes his head with a small smile as I shut my door. It was risky but worth it. For once, we have a little hope.

Chapter 18

"Tavvy and I were talking earlier," Ella says after barging into our room, where I'm clipping my cloak on, before she shuts the door. I'm not sure which one I'm more surprised about. That she and Tavvy have been talking, or that Ella is so happy so early in the morning. "And you need to drink this." Ella holds up a purple glittering vial that looks like that slime stuff that the kids in my neighbourhood had an obsession with the summer before I came here.

"I don't think anyone should drink that," I point out.

"It's magical protection against getting pregnant. You have a lot of boyfriends, and every girl here takes it," she says, and I want to be insulted about the "lot of boyfriends" comment, but she has a point.

"I've had it," Tavvy tells me. "It isn't all that bad."

"Why would you want it? You aren't dating anyone," I ask, only realising how harsh that might have sounded. "Sorry, I don't think I'm awake yet. I need more sleep."

"No worries, sleepy head, and it's just in case," Tavvy says, and she and Ella share a weird look.

"What am I missing?" I ask, placing my hands on my hips and glaring them both down. I can see the guilt a mile off.

"A lot, but we don't have time for all that now. Just drink it, and then we get going to fight class since they added an extra one this weekend due to the last lesson being a bit of a mess," Ella says, thrusting the vial at me. I pull the lid off, smelling it and finding out it smells like flowers. I close my eyes before taking a long drink, and the stuff burns my throat. I cough a few times, and Tavvy pats my back as Ella opens the door.

"It stops burning in a second," Tavvy explains as I straighten up and clear my throat a few times. I gratefully nod as the burn stops, and Tavvy goes to follow Ella out. I gently grab her wrist, stopping her from leaving.

"Are we okay?" I ask her because she has been weird with me recently.

"Yeah, we just need to talk—"

"Come on, slow coaches!" Ella interrupts, and I remind myself to bring this up with Tavvy again sometime as we walk out our room and down the corridor.

"Ella, Tavvy, don't you dare volunteer today. Let Mrs. Frostan choose who she is going to beat up," I warn my friends as we walk into fight class. It might be selfish, but they aren't fighting her. What I don't tell them as they nod at me is that I want to fight her instead. Her powers wouldn't stand a chance against mine, whereas she is challenged well against Ella and Tavvy and, well, most of the class, I think. Tavvy's fight proved to me that, in direct combat, she is hard to beat, so I'm going to use magic to do the most of it. We stop at the side of the group, and I look back to see Warren is stood by the door as Mrs. Frostan walks in, clicking those shoes against the ground. She keeps her head high as she moves to stand in front of us all, placing her hands on her hips. This time, she doesn't put a show on with her shadow copies or whatever the hell they are.

"Who is going to volunteer today?" she asks, and there is dead silence in the room. I almost expect a tumbleweed to roll past us any moment. Everyone else in fight class got to fight her shadows after we went back to our rooms with Tavvy, and I've heard they were easier to beat. They act like robots. The only one that is a risk is the boss woman herself, and no one wants to fight her.

"I will," I say, pushing my friends' hands away as they try to grab me with hushed whispers.

"Ah, I have heard such—"

"As her guard, I would like to challenge the student in your place." Warren shocks us all by stepping in, but it makes me almost smile. In his own way, he is protecting me. "You know of Miss Dormiens's powers and how it might be a little too easy for her to beat you."

"It wouldn't be easy," Mrs. Frostan says, getting all flustered as I keep my eyes on Warren.

"Then it shouldn't concern you if I step in," Warren retorts.

"Fine. It would be a good show to watch. Everyone, go and sit down out of the way," Mrs.

Frostan demands, clapping her hands together. I smile sweetly as I go and stand opposite where Warren stands in the middle of the room, his hand on his spear, and I wish I could see his expression.

"You surprised me, Warren Nightshade," I say, placing my hands at my sides and getting ready. They all want a show, and I'm sure not going down without a fight.

"I'm surprised you know my last name. Who told you?" Warren actually sounds surprised.

"That is a secret," I reply, grinning, and I wink once at him.

"I won't play nice, Miss Dormiens. I suggest you treat me as nothing more than an enemy," he gruffly tells me, and I watch as he places his spear right in front of him, placing both hands around the shaft. I can't see his face or hear the words I'm sure he whispers, but suddenly the glowing grey energy shoots up into the air and comes down around us like a dome. It completely blocks us from the outside; the grey is so dark that I can't see out of it. When I look back at Warren, he is gone, and the spear is standing on its own.

I call my magic as I spin around slowly,

watching in the darkness for anything. Thanks to my senses, I hear him to my left, and I turn around, flashing a shot of dust at him. Warren simply waves it away with grey energy, and I'm left shocked as I step back. I step back again, calling more dust, and I hold my hands out, pushing more of it towards him, but it does nothing. He covers himself in grey energy and walks through the dust until he is right in front of me. He knocks my hands away and steps closer, placing a finger under my chin.

"I win," he tells me, sounding smug.

"So do I," I reply and quickly pull his hood down before he can stop me. Wavy white hair curls around a very handsome face, with bright big eyes and a sexy jawline. He is my age, I think, but it takes me a second to realise why he didn't want me to see his face. A long, thick scar is drawn on his face diagonally. It is the shape of an *F*, and it is so big you can't miss it. The scar itself is odd; it's not red, it's blue. A direct clash against his skin, and it almost glows.

"Rueben Frostan did this to you, didn't he?" I say, gathering from the little Warren has told me about himself.

"I'm his. I've told you this already, but I didn't

want you to see me," he angrily says, dropping his hand.

"I think you are beautiful with the scar or without it. If anything, that scar makes me admire you more. You are braver than I ever thought. You shouldn't hide who you are, Warren," I tell him, knowing he likely doesn't want to talk to me. Warren surprises me by looking back and meeting my eyes. He very slowly lifts a hand to my cheek, frowning at me.

"No one has ever told me that. No one. I don't remember my mother to know if she thought I was beautiful, and my father never spoke to me much other than to say I looked like his sister who died as a child," he tells me.

"Warren, you are beautiful. Very much so. I'm sure you could win any girl's heart," I tell him, but the words feel so close to my heart as I speak them. I shouldn't be speaking to Warren like this or looking at him the way I am right now.

"What about yours?" he asks, and I'm shocked for a moment. I can't let him have my heart, not without telling the three men who already share it. I can't betray them, even if I want to kiss Warren. It's not fair. I wait until he is inches away from my lips before I place my hand over his mouth and call my power. He realises too late what I've done as he tries to fight off falling to sleep as he falls to the floor.

"W-why?" he asks as I pull his hood up, and I cheekily smile down at him.

"Sorry, I just really like to win." To my surprise, he laughs as his eyes begin to close. "But I meant what I said. It wasn't a trick," I add before he falls to sleep, and I can't help but smile. I think I really like Warren Nightshade.

Chapter 19

"You nearly died the last time you did this. We should say no," Warren says as I try to leave my room after he told me Rueben sent for me. He doesn't wear his hood down since I saw him, but he does push it back a little bit so I can see his eyes more as we talk, which is better than nothing. I know a lot of what he thinks is in his head, and that is a battle I can't fight for him. I try to push away the thoughts of his lips and how he looked at me.

"Is no actually an option when it comes to Rueben?" I ask, crossing my arms and raising an eyebrow at him. "I don't think it is, and neither do you. If I scream too much, pull me out, and then I can be healed with the Tale brothers later."

"I don't like this," Tavvy says, coming to my side. "I will get Quin; he needs to be there again. We need to make a plan soon, one that will get you out of here."

"Okay, thanks. I think I can handle it this time," I answer. Though Tavvy and Warren can see straight through the lie, if their simultaneous sighing is anything to go by. It's been four weeks since the last time Rueben called me to his office, and I honestly hoped he would never ask me to do this again. Since the books went missing, they have been madly searching the academy, and Warren told me he cancelled the lessons until further notice.

The Tale brothers and what is left of the good tale community are going stir crazy in that place, all of them desperate for contact with the outside world or to find family out there. We don't have a plan, and I'm no closer to the answers the people always ask for when I'm there. I can't tell them my own game plan is to wake the goddesses and ask for Sin's life back. It's a selfish move, because I know I should ask for her to save the world. We all stay silent as we pass a group of students, their dark tale guards following closely behind them.

"Without nearly dying?" Tavvy asks once the

corridor is silent and empty once again.

"Maybe...I don't know," I admit, remembering what Lane said about the raven stone. It should drain anyone that touches it, because it uses our energy for the power. So if I'm going down, I'm taking Rueben with me. He can pull us out of the vision and take the pain with it to boot.

"I won't watch you scream," Warren warns me and steps out of the way. We all walk to the stairs before Tavvy heads down the corridor, and it makes me wonder how she knows which room Quin is in. Tavvy has been quiet for the last couple of weeks here, but then again, this place would make anyone struggle. Ella is a ghost of herself, but Roger is doing a good job of keeping a close eye on her around the academy, so no guards have gone near. I never did see the guards that hurt Ella again though, and I know we all have Warren to thank for that.

I have Warren to thank for keeping me alive a lot of the time, and I still haven't been brave enough to really tell the Tale brothers about my feelings for Warren. I sat with Knox, Tobias and Noah all night yesterday, and somehow it works with us all, though the peace we have found relies highly on the success of Quin's mad plan working so the goddess can bring Sin back to us. We get outside the room, and instead of knocking, I go straight inside. Rueben is talking with a woman when I step into the room, but they soon go quiet and turn to face me.

"You must knock, Miss Dormiens," Rueben says and shakes his head as I tightly smile and look back for a second to see Warren close the door. "Never mind. This is Miss Fletcher, and she is a healer for the dark tales. I do not want you sick like last time, so Miss Fletcher will heal us both until we see what I want."

"I promise neither of you will die with me here," Miss Fletcher proudly states. I'm glad she has that much confidence in herself, but I certainly don't, considering I've never met her before this moment. I roll my eyes as I go and sit down on the chair and hold my hand out flat.

"Let's just get this over with. I don't want to chitchat," I say.

"Always straight to the point with you, Madilynn. I'm guessing you don't want a cup of tea then?" he asks, and I hate hearing him say my name. He always calls me Madilynn now, every time we pass in the corridors or when he creepily comes into class to stare at us.

"Not from you, no," I dryly respond. "I do have homework to do, so shall we get on with it?"

"Teenagers are always so fun to work with," Rueben jokes to Miss Fletcher, and she laughs. Dear god, how much this *teenager* wants to kill them both. Rueben finally pulls out the raven stone from his pocket and comes over. Miss Fletcher moves to stand right next to us as Rueben places the stone on my hand and covers it with his own. Seconds later, light blasts into my head, and I feel like it almost knocks me out until it disappears. I suck in a deep breath, even though my body instantly starts to hurt. I try to push the pain away, but it doesn't work as I really open my eyes to look around. We're back in the same room, but this time, one of the goddesses is passed out on the floor, and the other is in the arms of a man.

"If I do this, it means I will never see you again. Never hold you. Never kiss you," the man desperately tells her and kisses her. I can see they deeply love each other in this moment before she pushes him away to break free.

"If we don't do this, then the world ends. That is what she will do, I saw it," the goddess says. She is the one without the scar, the prettier of the two,

I think. Even though they are identical, there is something so special about her.

"Is there truly no other way?" a man asks. The man looks familiar to me as well; his blonde hair and build almost look like my father.

"I'm sorry, but you have to lock us away," she says and turns away, tears streaming down her cheeks as she goes to her sister. She picks her up and moves to stand on the stone platform where there are holes with markings all around it. The man pulls a bag off his shoulder and pulls out a bundle of daggers. He takes the six very recognisable daggers with jewel hilts out of the bag and goes to the statue. He starts pushing a dagger into the marked holes and turning them to the right. They light up, the stone on the hilt glowing brightly after he pushes each one in. He stops at the last one and looks up. The awake goddess waves a hand over her sister, who magically straightens to stand on her own, and holds her hands out. She holds her hand and looks once more at the man, with clear pain in her expression.

"I love you, I always will, but find another to love. It is your future. Have a life, my love. A real life, one that doesn't have big cost. I will always bless your line in spirit," the goddess says. "And only your blood will ever have the key."

"I love you. I always will, my goddess. My light. I will dream of you, forever," the man says, and the goddess smiles as he slides the last dagger into the space, and it glows red. The goddess looks up as the ground shakes a few times before the two goddesses turn into statues that look up at the ceiling.

The statue in the library. That is them, trapped like that forever, and they have been in the academy all this time.

"Oh my god," I whisper.

"Finally!" Rueben shouts in joy, but I feel nothing but horror as the vision fades away and I'm back in Rueben's office, gasping for air. Miss Fletcher has her hand on my arm and the other hand on Rueben's arm, but as I look at her, she is pale. A sickly pale, whereas I feel fine, and her eyes are frozen still.

"Thanks, we are back now, Miss Fletcher," I say, placing my hand over hers, which is freezing cold. She cries out only once before collapsing to the floor. I fall to the floor with her as Rueben steps away, gasping for air himself. I roll her onto her back and check her pulse, finding nothing there.

"Sh-she is d-dead," I stutter, standing up and wiping my hand like I can catch death or something. I know it's a silly thing to do, but I can't think straight as I stare at her. Seeing the goddesses has taken another life. How many lives am I willing to give up to bring Sin back? Can I even tell him I literally told the world to burn just so I could have him back? I look over at the window, where three ravens are flying in the air outside. They swoop in circles, round and round each other in an endless circle. I haven't seen Sin's soul since the funeral, but the ravens are always close. Always watching and waiting. They know I'm going to pay the price to bring Sin back. *Any price.*

"Never mind. We don't need to go back. I have daggers to look for," Rueben says, sitting at his desk and smiling at me. "Good work, Miss Dormiens. Now get out." I glare at him, feeling a sick sense of dread. I know he will look everywhere for those daggers, and funny enough, I know where all of them are.

And there is no way he is getting them. They are my last chance to save Sin's life.

Chapter 20

"I don't think they want me to come with you. You two should go, and I will stay here," Quin states, looking awkward as he leans against the door in our room. Tavvy is anxiously cleaning the room, something she only does when she is nervous. I know her well enough to figure out there is something going on that I'm missing. It's not just the cleaning right now...it's all the time lately. I would blame it on the stress of the academy and everything we are going through, but Tavvy is usually so strong. Right now, she is a mess, and I don't understand the actual reasoning behind it. Every time she looks at me, she parts her lips to say something before just deciding against it or walking away.

"Of course they don't want you there, but this is partly your plan, Quin. So you are coming with us, get over it," I tell him, still watching Tavvy.

"They won't hurt you or judge you any more than they already have done," Tavvy gently tells him, and they weirdly stare at each other. I go to ask them what the hell is going on with their strange eye contact thing when the portal appears. I don't wait for any of them as I walk straight through it and bump into Knox on the other side. He grins, wrapping his arms around my waist and lifting me off the ground as he picks me up and hugs me.

"I've missed you, Sleepy," Knox states as I lift my head and stare down at him. I admire how handsome he is up close for a moment before pressing my lips to his, only for a second.

"I've missed you too," I admit, and he smiles widely as he slides me slowly down his body, and I turn around just as Quin and Tavvy come through the portal. Knox links his fingers with mine as he locks eyes with Quin, and Tavvy awkwardly stands at his side, rubbing her arm with bright red cheeks.

"Why is he here?" Knox asks. All smiles and

kindness he had a moment ago are swiftly gone when he sees Quin standing right here.

"It's a long story. We need Tobias and Noah," I tell him.

"Tobias is down the river, on his usual run to burn off some energy," Noah smoothly says as he walks out of the corridor and into the room. Burn off energy means it is one of his coping mechanisms for his drug withdrawal problem. "We should talk and catch him later. Hey, Sleepy. You okay?" I nod and hold my other hand out as Noah comes over, linking his fingers with mine. It's a little odd to be holding both their hands, but considering they don't say anything, I'm not going to mention it. I like having them both near like this.

"Why don't we sit down?" Tavvy suggests as it gets more than awkward in here. We take seats on the sofa, with me sandwiched between Knox and Noah.

"So I used the raven stone again with Mr. Frostan—"

"You did fucking what?" Knox roars. "Have you got a death wish? You nearly died last time, and I cannot fucking lose you too." Knox gets off the sofa, and I gulp down the guilt he makes me feel.

"I'm sorry. I didn't have a big choice in the matter. If we don't find out where the goddesses are, then we *never* get Sin back," I remind him. "I will pay any cost to save him, you know that."

"Sin wouldn't want you to die a painful death to bring him back," Noah gently tells me, and I know that.

"Well, he isn't here to offer his opinion, so I did what I could, Noah," I remark and regret it the moment the words leave my lips. "I'm sorry, I didn't mean that. It isn't easy at the academy anymore, and it is starting to get to me. Everything from seeing the teachers slowly dying, to Ella being beaten and Tavvy nearly dying, to fight class being nothing more than a bloodbath that we are lucky no one has died in. I want Sin back, and then I want to get out of that place with everyone good."

"Are you okay?" Noah finally says, and I nod. Knox comes and sits back at my side. He doesn't say anything, but he links our fingers and holds our joined hands on his knee. It's enough. I know I'm not the only one finding it hard right now, and we just have to keep going.

"Mr. Frostan brought a dark tale healer in with us. Only she died keeping us alive," I explain.

"I'm sorry you had to see that," Knox tells me. I'm sorry she died, and I didn't even know her. She was so scared of letting Rueben down that she happily gave up her life for him. That's a lot of dedication to have. One thing is for sure, Rueben is loved by all of the dark tales at the academy from what I can tell.

"I didn't even really know her, and it sucks that I'm almost finding this normal now for the academy, for our life," I admit, and I try to ignore the looks of sympathy they all give me or the understanding I can see Tavvy feels. "Anyway, we found what we wanted. A way to bring the goddesses back."

"How?" Noah asks, and everyone is quiet as I explain it. I haven't even told Tavvy and Quinton the how or what I saw yet.

"The goddesses are the statues in the library, and the daggers, the ones we found, are the keys. Everyone is going to be looking for them. It's almost funny that we already know where they all are," I say, reaching into my cloak and pulling out a dagger, the one I kept with the blue stone.

Everyone is silent as we stare at the dagger, because no one really knows what to say. Somehow we found the keys all along, and it has been literally under our beds the whole time.

"Will Ella give you the last one? We have all ours here, in my room," Noah asks.

"Of course she will, and I will sneak into her room tonight to get it," I say.

"Then the next thing is that we need a distraction. A big one, because waking goddesses up is going to gain attention," Quin suggests.

"If we awake the good goddess, it means we wake the bad too," Tavvy says quietly into the room. "Is that a price everyone is willing to pay for Sin? She was bad, evil, and there must be a reason she is locked away with her sister."

"I will pay any price," I quickly say before anyone else can. I know it's crazy, I truly do, but crazier things have been done in the name of love. Possibly. Though awakening a crazy, evil old goddess to get Sin back might be near the top of that list.

"We all will pay the price, Sleepy," Knox interjects, and I nod.

"I owe Sin, and all of you. I will help and do anything I can to make this work," Quinton says.

"I know it won't make you forgive me or ever trust me again, but I have to start somewhere."

"I'm in too," Tavvy states. "You guys have quickly become like family to me, and I won't let you do this alone."

"Then what distraction did you have in mind, Quin?" I ask him and rest back in the seat as he starts explaining his idea. One way or another, we are getting Sin back. I won't rest until it happens.

*a*fter a long discussion between us all about a distraction, I leave Knox, Noah, Tavvy and Quinton alone to finish off the details. It should work, or at least I don't see any reason why it wouldn't. Now I want to tell Tobias, that is if I can find him first. I walk down the new stone paths between the houses made of stone, where I can hear people talking as soft light appears out of their windows.

I walk quickly to the end of the path, which curves out to the stream, where a guy is standing with his back to me, watching the water. His shirt is missing, so I can admire his toned back, the curve of every muscle and his tight waist. His dark, messy brown hair is lighter in some parts, looking like the very sun has kissed a boy destined for the moon. Moments like this, watching him when he doesn't know anyone is looking, are special because I really see him. Not the Tobias who struggled all this time. Not the Tobias who was lost in grief and pain. I see him and how beautiful he is. How calm and alluring and safe. I take a step closer, which alerts him to the fact I'm here, and he turns his head back to see me, a big smile slowly appearing on his face.

"Madilynn Dormiens, how lovely it is to see you here," he teases me, holding a hand out for me to take when I get close.

"Tobias Tale, it is lovely to see you as well," I tease right back as I take his hand, and he tugs me against his chest. My one hand goes to right above his heart, where there is the same z tattoo that they all have.

"Why do you all have a z tattoo on your torsos?" I ask him, running my finger over the z, and he shivers under my hand.

"It's for you. When we had to leave you, we wanted a reminder who owns our hearts and always will. The z is because it reminds us of our sleepy girl," he gently tells me, his cheeks looking a little pink as I can sense he is a little embarrassed to tell me that. My heart beats fast as I smile widely at him. Instead of saying anything, I move my hand to the side and lean my head down, pressing a kiss to the tattoo. I feel his heart beating so fast under my lips for that second, and when I look up, I see nothing but a fire burning in his eyes.

"I love you, Tobias Tale," I admit to him. Tobias slowly slides his hands into my hair, before placing his lips inches away from mine as we stare at each other. I nervously stand still, hoping he feels the same way as I do. I'm sure he does, but I need to hear it. I need Tobias close now more than ever before.

"I have always loved you. I knew it the moment you fell off your bike when we were eight and you cried in my arms. I knew even then that how I felt for you was different from anything else. It was real, it was special, and I lost track of that for a while until you found me again. Now I will never lose track of us again. I will fight for us, and I will love you forever if you will have me. I don't mind that you love my brothers; I know we aren't the normal kind of love, and that is okay with me. I just want you like I always have done," I stop him before he can say anything else by kissing him and throwing my arms around his neck. Tobias growls into my mouth as he picks me up, grabbing my ass tightly as I press myself into him more. Tobias carries me to the side of a building, pressing me against it as he arches his body into mine.

"We could get caught here," I say, even though part of me likes the danger.

"You're right," Tobias mumbles against my lips, moving one of his hands from my ass to slide up my chest. "Want to go inside?" I find myself only able to nod, and he carries me off the wall. I only look back as Tobias kicks a door open and lets me down in a small storage room. The walls are lined with food, bottles of water, and blankets. I grab a few of the blankets, laying them down on the floor as Tobias shuts the door, and he locks it. There isn't much light in here now, just the dim sunlight coming through the small windows at the top of the room.

Neither of us says anything, because there is nothing to say as we stare at each other. Feeling brave, I unclip my cloak, letting it fall to the floor on the blanket. I gather the bottom of my shirt, pulling it up over my head and loving the way

Tobias looks at me. How his eyes drift over all of my bare skin, like he is committing it to memory. I want to tell him he doesn't need to do that; I'm his, and I will be for a long time. I want us to have forever.

I slowly push my leggings off before stepping out of them and feeling quite nervous as he walks over to me, kicking off his shoes as he does. The joggers he is wearing are low on his hips, only really held up by his hip bones.

"I love you, I really fucking do, Sleepy," Tobias tells me as he lowers me to the floor, and then he kisses me. I moan as he presses his body on top of mine as he devours my mouth, and all sense of anything but Tobias is swiftly gone. Tobias kisses his way down my jaw to my neck and then to my breasts. He unclips my bra at the front before pushing it out of the way as he kneels between my legs. The way he looks at me in this moment is perfect. It does wonders for the ego because he looks at me like I'm the best present he has ever had.

I moan as he runs his fingers over my nipples, making them hard as steel, which he seems to like. Keeping one hand on my breast, teasing my nipple, he slides the other hand down between my legs. I chuckle as he rips my panties off like they are nothing and chucks them to the side.

He soon makes my laugh turn into moans as he uses his fingers to make everything feel amazing. Tobias sure knows what he is doing. My back arches as an orgasm slams into me, making everything blurry as I feel Tobias move his hand away and climb onto me, pressing his length into my core. I kiss him as he slides inside me in one smooth movement, which feels incredible. A pleasure-filled sigh escapes my lips because I feel like this was always meant to be. Tobias thrusts in and out of me, hard and fast, drawing out both our pleasure as he kisses me. He only slows down towards the end, lifting his head and making sure to keep his eyes locked onto mine as he comes.

"God, Sleepy," he gasps against my lips. I hold him as close and as tightly as he holds me back. Tobias and I might have had a difficult time to get to this point, but I know there is no way I'm letting him go now. He pulls out of me and cuddles up close. There is no sound but our breathing as we lie together, and no words are needed. We just needed each other.

Chapter 21

"What do you think?" Tavvy asks, smoothing down the dark green dress she has on. It is breathtakingly stunning, especially against her pale skin and long curly blonde hair that flows around her shoulders. Quinton's idea of a ball to celebrate our findings of the goddess went down well with Rueben, who happily agreed, because it meant his goons could spend more time exploring the rooms of the students while they weren't in them. The last week has been nothing but dark tales barging into rooms, emptying bags, and searching the entire academy for the daggers. Unfortunately for Rueben, all the daggers are in Knox's dimension and safe from them until tonight.

"Gorgeous," I tell her as I stand up in my sparkling blue dress. It's all lacy at the top, the lace stretching down my arms and stopping at my wrists. My hair is all curled like Tavvy's, and it's so long now that it hits the middle of my back. We look like fairy tales or at least the dresses the princesses used to wear. "Tavvy, why do I feel like there is something you are hiding from me? You've been so weird with me recently. Have I upset you?"

"No, of course you haven't. You're my bestie and always will be...but I think you might hate me," she nervously says.

"Why?" I ask, totally confused as she looks close to tears.

"I kissed Quinton, and he kissed me back. I don't know when it happened exactly, but I think it was when he saved my life. I fell in love with him somewhere along the line, and he told me he feels the same," she blurts out to me and just stares at me as I try to process what she just said. I guess a part of me kind of knew, because neither of them is good at hiding the little looks and just the way they are around each other all of the time.

"Oh," I quietly whisper. I'm too shocked to

say anything else or stop her rambling as she comes closer to me and takes my hands in hers. I don't pull my hands away though. I don't actually feel upset like I think I'm meant to.

"But best friends don't date their bestie's ex-boyfriend. Especially when it is super complicated between you two still. I told him this, and I'm sorry anything ever happened. It shouldn't have," she rambles on. "I love you like a sister and that means so much to me. You are the sister I never had, and I really mean that."

"Hold up, you ended it?" I ask her.

"Yes, because you're my bestie and—"

"Sit down," I say, waving a hand at the chair, and she looks confused as she goes and sits. I sit on the other chair in the room, right next to her, and take her hand in mine.

"The moment I left for Lost Time Academy, anything Quin and I had was gone. It was well and truly slammed into the dirt many times *after* that, while we are on it. I care about him because we grew up as friends and had a relationship. Our relationship wasn't true love though. I didn't know it at the time, but I do now," I say, trying to explain this to her. "The way I feel about the Tale brothers, *that* is real. I would rather die than be sent to some school to be away from them. I *never* felt that way with Quinton. If anything, somewhere deep down, I was okay to leave and end it. I felt like I was just saying goodbye to a best friend, not the love of my life. Anyways, we were kids back then, and things were easy. The moment it got difficult and hard choices had to be made, it wasn't Quinton I wanted at my side. I will always love him in a way, and if you can accept my friendship with him, I have no right to stand in the way of your relationship."

"Really?" she asks, wiping tears from her eyes, and I do the same as I shakily nod.

"Love is usually messy and unexpected, but we live in a dark, fucked up world. We should grab every chance of happiness and love that we can and hold on tight," I say to her. "And I love you as a sister, Tavvy. I love my Tale brothers, and this world we are in has taught me love is so rare and can be taken so quickly."

"I love you too, bestie," she says, hugging me tightly before letting go and looking at the door. "I told Quin I wouldn't be his date tonight to the ball, but he said he would just go alone without me."

"Go and get him," I say, pulling her up to stand at the same time I do.

"Are you sure?" she nervously asks. I pull her into another hug, making sure she understands.

"I love you, bestie. Now go and get your man," I whisper to her, and I can feel her beaming smile and happiness before she turns around and opens the door. Tavvy is as shocked still as I am at the sight of Warren outside the door, his hand raised to knock the door. The cloak is gone, replaced with a tight-fitting black tux, and what is more shocking is that he isn't hiding his face. His white hair has been cut, styled back out of his eyes but still holding some of that wavy quality. I can tell he is nervous as he lowers his hand, and I smile at him. The scar does nothing but make him more handsome, more different and special in my eyes. I love how brave he is in this moment. His spear is diagonally strapped to his back by a holder. My handsome guard.

"Unexpected, huh?" Tavvy teases me, and I shake my head, snapping out of the strange staring thing I was doing. You know, gawking like a total loser. Tavvy waves goodbye to me, mouthing "thank you" as she goes, and heads off to find Quinton. I should feel weird about my bestie and my ex-boyfriend hooking up, but it doesn't feel that way. I know Tavvy, and it must be real to make her like she is. Tavvy is one of the strongest people I know, and she wouldn't fall in love with just anyone. She is also loyal, and I know it must have been eating her up inside to break up with him before it even started and not tell me.

I also understand why she didn't want to tell me; we have a lot of dangerous things going on and need to keep our eyes on the game. Talking of which, I haven't told Warren any of the plan. I don't know who he is going to side with when it truly comes down to it. How he looks at me right at this moment, makes me have hope he might choose my side. I don't know though, or I do and that scares me.

"It seems you need a date to a ball," Warren says, leaning against the door frame and crossing his arms. Somehow this just makes him look even sexier.

"Are you my dark prince then?" I tease.

"Yes," he simply replies, but it means so much more, and we know it. I clear my throat and walk out the room, hooking my arm through his before we walk down the corridor. There is light music playing, though it isn't like the last ball I went to.

That was light and fun and everything good in the world. This ball is dark, seductive and cold. It only has one true purpose: to celebrate darkness. But what Rueben doesn't know is that he is being played. As we dance around the ballroom, the Tale brothers and the fighters have been going around the academy with bags of my sleeping dust that I made for them, putting the dark tale guards to sleep, one by one, until they take control of the library and set off the signal.

I smile widely at Rueben who stands outside the room to the dining hall, where the ball is going on behind him. We are a little later than everyone else, but I planned it that way. Rueben's eyes quickly drift over me, but they stayed fixed on Warren, clear shock in his eyes as he takes in the fact Warren isn't hiding anymore. We walk past him, but he catches Warren's other arm, stopping him.

"Remember your place, boy," Rueben darkly warns Warren before letting go.

"He knows his place, Mr. Frostan," I reply, and Warren just looks down at me with a small smile. Warren doesn't reply or look at me again as we carry on into the ball. I see Ella straightaway —her dark red dress isn't hard to miss with her long red hair flowing around her as Roger spins her around. What I'm sure was nothing more than a friendship based off Ella's need for protection, seems to have turned into so much more than that. I look up at Warren as he looks down at me at that moment, just as a new song comes on. A slow, romantic song I really like.

"Will you dance with me, Madi?" he softly asks, and I take a deep breath before I nod once. I can't let myself fall for him. Not in this moment. Not with this dance. We are at war, and Warren is lost somewhere in the middle of it. I can't trust that his side is firmly with me, and not with his loyalty to or fear of Rueben. But for one moment, I let him take me to the dance floor and hold me close as we sway to the music. The lyrics speak of lost moments, of love being found in the most unusual places, and it speaks about us far more than I want to admit. This moment must be lost, because what else could there be?

"You seem deep in thought," he whispers to me. "What is going on in your mind? I can't read you tonight."

"When I see you, the real you, it hurts. It hurts because looking at you is like looking at fire. I can't get close because, under the beauty, the

seduction and longing...loving fire is just dangerous," I honestly tell him what I've been thinking. I
shouldn't have said a word, and we both know it.

"Who said fire always has to burn?" he tells
me. "When you are two of the same soul, it is
impossible to burn the other without destroying
yourself."

"Warren," I gently warn him.

"Tonight we will dance and smile and be
everything your plan needs. Tomorrow, when the
war is over, we can talk about the future," he tells
me, and my eyes widen as I look at him.

"How did you know?" I quietly ask.

"I had an unexpected visit from Quinton last
night. He wanted to check whose side I am on,"
he tells me. I'm surprised Quin did that.

"And whose side *are* you on, Warren?" I ask.

"Yours and whoever you decide to follow," he
tells me, and before I can answer, he spins me out
and pulls me back to him. I rest my hands on the
back of his neck and place my head on his
shoulder.

"I have three—possibly four if this plan works
—other boyfriends. It's complicated, and you
should run the other way before they find out," I

tell him, because once tonight is over, I'm sitting them all down and explaining it all anyway.

"I will tell them with you. You haven't betrayed them, Madi, so they have no reason to be angry," he reminds me.

"Oh, they will be angry," I mutter, but I feel a little better that Warren hasn't run away now he knows all the facts. I look across the ball, and that's when I see them. Quin and Tavvy dance together, holding each other closely and looking at each other. I imagine it's how Sin and I looked at the last ball as we danced together. I expected to feel mad or even jealous seeing them together, but at this moment, I feel nothing but joy for the love they have found for each other.

"HELP!" someone screams, running into the room, and the music is cut off, plunging the ball into silence. I push through the crowd to find Mrs. Frostan on her knees, sleeping dust on her shirt like someone just missed her face with it. Rueben runs over to her, just as she says the last thing I want her to before she passes out on the floor.

"The Tale brothers are here. They are taking over the academy!"

Chapter 22

"GUARDS!" Rueben shouts as Quin, Tavvy, Ella and Roger get to my side. We hold a strong line as the rest of the students run to the back of the room, keeping out of the way. They can't help us right now, and I want Rueben's attention to be on us.

"It's too late," I shout at Rueben, catching his attention, and he looks at me in shock. I fill my hands with dust, but I don't get a chance to use my powers as Knox walks into the room.

"You are going to pay for taking Oisin Tale's life." Knox's arms are a swirl of impressive powers, a mixture of fire, water, electricity and air all swirling together. Rueben laughs, a cold empty laugh that makes me shiver as I watch how Knox moves. He is determined, powerful, and he will end this once and for all. I didn't know he had such control over all elements, though he told me it was possible.

Rueben strikes first, slamming five daggers of ice towards Knox. My heart is in my mouth as Knox simply knocks each one away, all the time walking forward. The air feels like it is slowly sucked out of the room as Knox and Rueben fight, a true show of elemental power that is frightening. Rueben holds his hands out, sending a storm of snow and deadly ice spikes towards Knox, who counters with a shield of fire. The shield covers him as he walks all the way through the storm, and I can't see him anymore. I hear the elements though, and the room becomes so cold that my breaths come out like smoke.

"Quinton, go and help him, please," Tavvy demands, but I can tell she doesn't want him to go, even though we both know he has more of a chance of saving Knox than we do. Quin nervously nods at her before letting go and running head first into the storm. I watch as Tavvy's skin lights up with green dust, and it makes her hair float around her, sparkling. She looks to me, nodding once. It's time we head to the library.

"We should get to the library," Ella says, making sure the others know. Roger looks back to the people and to us, and I know he needs to stay to protect them.

"Not until I know Knox is okay," I say, and I don't look his way as I try to see through the storm, but it's pointless. I can only hear them in there shouting and fighting. I doubt sending any sleeping dust towards them will help at this point; the storm is too large, and I can hardly look at it. Seconds later, the storm instantly disappears, and I run forward, seeing that Quin has frozen his uncle to the ground in a solid ice block. Knox is holding a spear made of pure fire and staring down at Rueben.

"It will hold him for a bit. Long enough to do what we need to," Quin explains to us.

"I should kill him now," Knox spits out.

"No. Let us get Sin back, and then he can be publicly killed as we end the war. This isn't the time," I tell Knox, who looks from Rueben to me. I lock eyes with him as he rages a war in his mind not to end Rueben's life now. As he makes the spear disappear, a part of me suspects I might just regret this decision one day.

"Let's go," Knox says, taking my hand. Ella quickly decides to tell the remaining students what to do while we wait for her by the door.

"Everyone stay here and lock the door, protect yourselves," Ella commands them, and she kisses Roger before running off to us.

"Can we trust him?" Knox asks as Warren stays by my side.

"Yes. I promise," I tell Knox, who doesn't seem to like it, but he carries on leading us out of the dining room. We run past dozens of knocked out students to the stairs to the library before running down them as fast as we can. We find Noah and Tobias in the library with all the lights on, and they have pushed the benches out of the way. All the daggers but one are in the right places, and Noah is holding the last one.

"You should do it," Noah says, placing the dagger in my hand when I get to him.

"Everyone else should stand back, just in case," I suggest, feeling nervous as I look up into the faces of the goddess statue. I know we shouldn't be doing this, I can feel it, but then I think of Sin. I want him back. At any cost. Before I can think on it more, I find the last gap and slide the dagger in, turning it to the side. It clicks, but the stone doesn't light up like the rest of them are doing.

"Why isn't it working?" I ask. I run around the statue, checking all the daggers are pressed in and not finding a problem. *This has to work.*

"Is there anything written on it?" Warren asks, walking over and looking around the statue with me.

"Who is that?" Noah asks as he comes over and helps to search.

"Warren Nightshade. I'm Madi's friend," Warren introduces himself, and Noah shakes his outstretched hand. The tense way they both are standing indicates their internal battle not to kill each other. But I'm getting the feeling that the more we are around dark tales, the more it doesn't bother us.

"You call her Madi?" Tobias asks, coming to Noah's side.

"We don't have time for this, everyone look and see—" I pause when I find a sentence written, but it isn't in English or anything I can read. I think it's Latin, and I did not pay attention in that class one tiny bit.

"Can anyone read this?" I ask them.

"There is someone coming down the stairs!" Ella shouts to us from the door as Warren gets to my side and reads the sentence out loud in English.

"Only the children of tales can be the key. Hold the key and say Dormiens."

"My last name? Why would it——" I stop as Ella sends two dark tales flying out the door, the sound of their heads slamming again the stairs is heard not long after. Tavvy runs to her side with Quin, who quickly puts up a wall of ice at the bottom of the stairs to stop anyone getting in.

"I think we need to hold a dagger each, and then say my last name to open it," I tell everyone, hearing the shouts and the ice being chipped away. It won't be long before they get in.

"Six people need to do it, and two people need to guard the door," Ella points out, working it all out quicker than the rest of us have. "I'm going to guard the door. I've decided it."

"And I'm going to help her," Tavvy says, looking to Ella, and they hold hands for a moment.

"Not without me, you're not," Quinton says as Tavvy and Ella look to me. I nod once, tears falling down my cheeks because we all know what it means. They are my best friends, and I know we need to do this. We need six people, or this isn't going to work.

"Ella and I are well suited to fight together. You need to do this, to make up for the past. I know you need to do this," Tavvy tells Quin and then kisses him like they are saying goodbye. It's hard to watch, because I don't want to see them say goodbye to each other. I can see how real it is. And real is hard to find.

"Well that's new," Tobias mumbles, and Noah mutters something similar. Knox just looks to me, and I nod at him.

"Be careful," I tell Tavvy when she looks my way once more as she lets Quin go. I look at Ella for a moment to make sure she knows I mean both of them. "We won't be long, hopefully, then we can all get out of here." No one says anything else as we each go to a dagger. Ella and Tavvy close the doors, and only seconds later, we hear them fighting. It's seconds later until there is screaming, and I'm desperate to go to them when the scream sounds painful.

Quin goes to move to the door, but Knox grabs his arm, pushing him back to the dagger.

"No," he warns Quin. His tears match mine as I grip the dagger tightly, knowing I have to do this.

"Dormiens!" I shout. Noah, Tobias, Knox, Warren and Quin say it just after me, and the stones on the daggers start to glow. I cry out as I'm blasted away from the statue by what felt like a gust of wind. I slam into the wall, scraping my arm and ripping my dress as a bookcase crashes onto me. I climb out from under it, gasping from the pain as I hear a loud bang. The ground harshly shakes as I pick myself up from the ground, seeing Knox right next to me while everyone else was also blasted away. I look to the goddesses just as the stone fades from the tip of their heads all the way down to their white dresses. Everything just pauses as we stare at them, and then in the blink of an eye, one of the goddesses slides a black dagger out from her pocket and stabs the other before disappearing.

"NO!" I shout, running over to the platform where the goddess has fallen to her knees, thick blood pouring from her stomach. I climb onto the platform as everyone surrounds us, and I kneel in front of her, pulling her onto my lap. No one should die alone.

"What is your name?" I ask her.

"Avalon," she tells me.

"I'm Madi," I gently reply to her, and it's hard not to stare at how simply beautiful she is, a true goddess.

"I might be able to heal—" Warren starts to suggest.

"No, dark prince. This is not a wound my kind can ever survive. The dagger is a soul dagger, born in the fire I was created in," she gently tells him, and I have no clue how exactly she knows who Warren is, let alone what I called him.

"How can we help?" I ask.

"You need me to help you. One more time, I will bless the Dormiens line. I loved your ancestor, and for him, I will do this," she tells me. A tear runs down my cheek when I see how pale she is, how she is struggling to tell me anything.

"I didn't even ask..." I whisper.

"You want to save someone, bring them back from the dead. That I cannot do," she honestly tells me, though her words make me cry. Screams of pain come from the other side of the door, and Avalon holds her hand up, placing a wall of light that looks like water in front of the doors to stop anyone getting in.

"Oh," I say, placing my hand over my heart as a deep pain burns in it. Tavvy and Ella might be seriously hurt, Sin can't come back, and this all was for nothing.

"We should go and help—"

"The tale girls are dead now. You cannot help them," the goddess tells us. A sob leaves my lips as Quin shouts and runs to the door. He falls to his knees, crying, but everyone else is just silent.

"I will send you back in time," the goddess says.

"What?" I ask, wiping my tears away.

"I have enough power to send you six back to the moment Oisin was hurt and this future happened. The versions of you that exist in the past will disappear the moment you appear, so you must be ready for that. Lost Time Academy is called that because I once saw a vision of you, Madilynn Dormiens. You need time to be lost to save the world. I will help you. It is the last thing I will do," she tells me. "Then you can find the end of the prophecy and fulfill it. The world will be whole and perfect as it should be once again."

"Thank you," I whisper to her, as I'm completely unsure what else to say.

"You must promise me one more thing,

Madi," Avalon says. "Come closer so I can whisper it." I lean down, placing my ear near her lips as she asks me to do one big thing. I don't get to tell her yes before the world burns away into a light, and the last thing I hear before I fall into it is Avalon saying goodbye.

Chapter 23

hen I open my eyes, every part of my body burns, right down to my soul, as I gasp for air and try to calm my breathing down. My heart is beating so fast as my eyes are blurry, but the night sky is clear above me. The air is freezing cold, and I slowly become aware of the cold grass underneath me as I stretch out my hands. We are outside, and it is seriously freezing cold. Ravens screech in the distance, and I groan as I try to sit up. Someone wraps an arm under me, lifting me up, and I see it's Warren now that things are a little less blurry.

"It worked?" I ask, looking around and not seeing anyone.

"There!" Noah shouts, pointing into the distance where two hooded figures are carrying Sin's body into the woods. Quin shoots two blasts of ice, freezing the hooded figures, who drop Sin to the floor as ice crawls up their bodies and they shout until they are frozen. We can't be too late. I'm running with them all until we get to where Sin lies. I stand still as Knox places his hands on Sin's chest before they start glowing from the power.

"He's alive," Knox gasps, absorbing some of his twin's wound. "I can't heal all of it but enough to keep him alive." I rest my hand on Sin's cheek and cry from the pure feel of him alive. We did it, and my heart finally can breathe again. I drop my head as a pure relieved laugh leaves my lips, and tears drop onto the icy ground below.

"I can heal him fully, but not out here," Warren explains, and Knox looks to me, his eyes burning with power.

"He is really alive?" I whisper, thick tears streaming down my cheeks.

"Yeah, Sleepy. We did it," he says, and I lean closer, wiping his tears away before stepping back, because I can celebrate with them later. I have a promise to keep. A promise in exchange for this gift. Sin is back, and there is a tiny chance we can all have a happy ending for once.

It's a chance I will give everything for.

"Warren, please don't let my dust put you guys to sleep. Saving the world alone would be difficult," I tell him as I start to walk backwards, away from them.

"What are you talking about?" Noah asks, but Warren nods in agreement.

"I made a promise, and you must not stop me," I explain to them all, looking one more time at Sin and smiling widely, feeling so happy it almost hurts my face to smile so much. I turn around and run into the field. I stop roughly in the middle and hold my hands out at my side. I'm not exactly sure how to do this, but if Avalon said I could, then I'm going to try to.

"I am Madilynn Dormiens, and everyone shall sleep." I say the words Avalon told me, before pulling every inch of power I can possibly find into myself. I feel my feet leave the ground as the power begins to hurt, to burn into my soul and make my body ache to stop doing it. I cry out as my head flings back and my hands go to my chest. I hear my name being screamed, but I can't stop this.

It's my destiny.

It's my promise.

It's my fairy tale, and it's just the beginning.

Epilogue

Warren

"MADI!" Noah shouts, looking up in wonder like us all. All of our shouting has done nothing to distract her, and I have a feeling we shouldn't anyway.

I use my spear to make a dome of grey energy around us, protecting this little group and making sure I can see Madi all the time. She floats into the air, and very suddenly, wings appear behind her made of pure blue dust. They are massive, twice the size of her, and they spread out. She looks like a fairy princess from a damn fairy tale.

"Anyone else seeing the wings? Did anyone

know she could do that?" Tobias asks in pure shock.

"Nope," Noah answers, sounding just as shocked. Suddenly she slams her arms out, and ravens fly out of her, hundreds of them all in one go. They are made of pure blue dust and they spread it as they fly out in all different directions. They leave massive piles of dust in their wake, heading straight for us.

"What is she doing?" Knox asks, standing over his brother.

"I think she is putting the entire island to sleep. Every single tale in a deep sleep. Just like the raven prophecy said," Quin answers in awe, and I know he is right. Madilynn is the most powerful tale out there, and no one ever saw it. I wait until the ravens are gone before lowering the dome and running towards her. Just as she collapses, I jump up and catch her in mid-air before she falls. I place my finger on her neck, feeling a pulse and knowing she has just overdone herself. Her Tale brothers and Quin run over, except for Knox who slowly walks, holding his brother in his arms.

"Is she okay?" Tobias asks first, but then his tone soon changes as I nod. "Hand her over."

Because I don't want to cause an argument, I carefully hand Madi over to Tobias who I can see is very protective. I've got a long way to go if I want these guys to trust me. One thing is for certain. I want to be around Madi in any way I can be. I've never met anyone like her, and she is worth fighting for.

"She is alive and just tired, I suspect," I answer.

"What do we do now?" Noah asks, stroking some of the hair out of her eyes. It's clear they love her, and I don't know how my love for her can even compare.

"I know where we should go," Knox says and opens a portal with a click of his fingers. I look back at the academy and hear the pure silence. No bird whistles, no person talks, and there is no sound but the wind.

Madilynn Dormiens just put the tales world to sleep...but what happens when they wake up?

PRE-ORDER TALES & DARKNESS HERE...

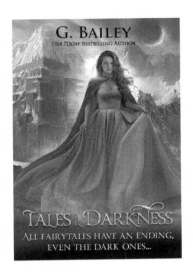

Thank you so much for reading Tales & Dreams!! A big thank you to Helayna, Mads, Cora and everyone that supported me with this book! Including my wonderful Pack Leaders <3

A special thank you to my family. Without you, I couldn't be who I am today and my books wouldn't exist. You are everything.

Book three, Tales & Darkness, will is on Pre-order for August the 1st <3

Thank you for your continued support! You're all amazing!

Link to Tales & Darkness…

Instagram

Facebook

Twitter

Pinterest

Sign up to my Newsletter for teasers,

giveaways and more...

Sign up here.

www.gbaileyauthor.com

About the Author

G. Bailey is a USA Today bestselling author of books that are filled with everything from dragons to pirates. Plus, fantasy worlds and breath-taking adventures. Oh, and some swoon-worthy men that no girl could forget. G. Bailey is from the very rainy U.K. where she lives with her husband, two children and three cheeky dogs. And, of course, the characters in her head that never really leave her, even as she writes them down for the world to read!

Please feel free say hello on here or head over to Facebook to join G. Bailey's group, Bailey's Pack! (Where you can find exclusive teasers, random giveaways and sneak peeks of new books on the way!)
FIND MORE BOOKS BY G. BAILEY ON AMAZON... LINK HERE.

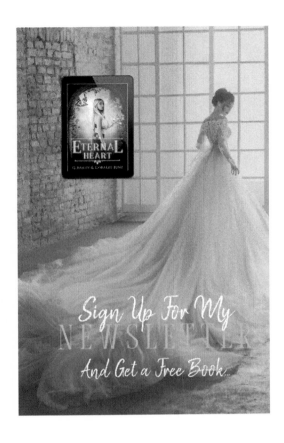

Sign Up For My
NEWSLETTER
And Get a Free Book...

Click here....

Ever heard the saying "Never follow the big bad wolf into the woods"?

Well, I wish I had listened to Little Red Riding Hood's advice.

One bite. That's all it took to turn Harper into a wolf and change her entire life. Turning eighteen was meant to be a fun night out, a party in the woods to celebrate with friends, but it ends in disaster. Harper wakes up in a car on her way to a pack of wolves— ones she must live with.

The sexy and alluring alpha welcomes her, declaring her his mate. Only Harper's best friend, a vampire she grew up with, tells her she belongs with him. Now, Harper must keep her mates from destroying each other.

To make matters worse, the wolves are at war with other kinds of shifters. When one of them turns up, demanding she is his mate, will her alpha who she rejected fight for her?

Will the vampire who loves her help her wolf pack?

18+ ménage. This is a short series, filled with fairy-tale re-telling stories with a lovely HEA!

24

Harper

"*R*eally? A party in the woods? That's where you want to spend your eighteenth birthday?" Colton asks me, just as the school bell rings, signalling the end of class and the last day of school for us. It's finally over, and to celebrate, everyone is going to this party in the woods tonight. Well, everyone except Colton, that is, and he hasn't stopped asking me why I want to go, since I told him this morning of my plans. I chuck my books in my bag, looking around at all my classmates as they run out the door, all of them so happy to leave.

"Yes, why won't you come?" I ask, pulling my coat on and picking up my bag. He grins at me—

a cheeky grin that matches his personality. Colton is every bit the typical hot guy in looks, with short blond hair, bright blue eyes, and golden skin. In fact, when he spoke to me for the first time last year, I choked on my drink and blurted out a load of words that made no sense. While I was utterly mortified, he still wanted to be my friend. He's a strange guy, but we quickly became best friends.

"I just can't, not at night," he mutters, pushing a hand through his hair. It's a nervous tick of his.

"You know, I never see you out at night. Are your parents really that strict?" I ask. He always leaves my house before the sun sets, and he never wants to go out after school in the winter because it gets dark so quickly. I met his parents once, and they didn't like me; at least, I don't think they did, considering they never replied to me when I said hello, and only asked Colton what he was doing bringing me home with him.

"Something like that." He smiles, but it almost seems a little sad. "Let's go and get some lunch. I have a gift for you," Colton says and holds his hand out for me. I take it as we leave the classroom.

"Why do you always hold my hand, Colt?" I

ask him, and he smiles down at me as we stroll through the nearly empty corridors.

"I want to, it's that simple," he says and shrugs his shoulders.

"You should hold hands with a girlfriend, not me. This is why you don't have one." I lift our joined hands, and he laughs.

"I don't have one because I don't want one, Harper." He nudges my shoulder. "Plus, every girl here is too scared of you to try and hit on me."

"What eighteen-year-old guy doesn't want a girlfriend? And I'm not that bad." I laugh.

"This one. And yes, you are. You glare at them when they speak to me," he says. To be fair, I don't exactly glare. It's just, the Barbie dolls that try to hit on Colton aren't good enough for him. Colton needs a sweet girlfriend, someone kind and not made of mostly plastic. I roll my eyes and stop as Skye runs up to us in the car park. Skye is my only other friend in this school, in this village. Growing up in foster care isn't easy; bouncing from house to house isn't any better. When I moved here last year, no one would talk to me until I met Skye. And then I met Colton.

"Harper, are you still coming tonight?" she

asks, stopping in front of me, not even looking at me as she talks. No, her eyes are on Colton. Not that he even looks her way, he never has. Skye has tried to get me to set her up with him on several different occasions, but I don't know how many times I've told her that he isn't interested. I do get her interest, even I have to admit Colton is extremely good-looking compared to the guys at this school. Or any school I've ever been to, for that matter.

"Yeah, I will meet you there at eight." I smile at her, even though I'm getting annoyed at how she acts around Colton. I roll my eyes as she twirls her blonde hair around her finger and steps closer to him.

"Are you coming, Colt? I know I would love to see you there," she says, her words laced with suggestion. She may as well strip down naked and lay herself out for him at this rate.

"No, it's Harper's birthday, and I have plans for her. See you around, Skye," he says, tugging on my hand as she frowns. I give her a small smile as I walk past her with Colt and get into his SUV. Colt has a Land Rover, a red one he fixes himself. The vehicle runs like a dream, and the inside has dark blue leather seats he custom fitted in here. They're even heated.

"Urgh, I wish I had your car," I say as I snuggle down in the seat and clip my seat belt on.

"I would give you anything, Harper, but not my car." He winks at me, and I laugh. Colt makes sure his seatbelt is latched before turning on the car to drive us the ten minutes out of town. I smile and lean back in my seat when I see where he is driving us to.

"The water tower?" I ask him.

"Where else? We always go there when we want to be alone," Colt says, and I turn the heat on for the seats.

"Alright, anything is better than going back home," I comment.

"What did she say?" Colt asks, picking up straight away that my foster parent has done something.

"The usual—she wants me to move out, but it's still difficult to hear on your eighteenth birthday, you know?" I try not to think of my foster mum and how she needs me to move out, as she doesn't get paid to look after me anymore. Every foster home I've been in has been about the money, and they want a child that they basically don't have to deal with. There isn't one I can remember being loving. I've been in foster care for as long as I remember, since I lost both my parents, but I was too young to remember their deaths. I don't even have photos or anything from them, as it was all sold or lost over the years. I wonder if I look like them as I see my reflection in the window; my big green eyes, my long brown hair, and my pale skin. I wonder what parts of my face look like my mum or dad.

"You could come and live with me," Colt tells me, snapping me out of my thoughts.

"I'm sure your parents would love that. They don't like me, remember?" I chuckle.

"They don't get you; it's not that they don't like you. I can't explain it, but trust me, they wouldn't say no. I won't see you out on the streets, Harper," he says, resting his hand on my knee for a second and squeezing it.

"I know you wouldn't." I smile at him as he returns his hand to the wheel. Colton pulls onto the old road, where the water tower sits at the end. The tall fixture hasn't been used in years; it was just left here and looks like it's close to falling apart. Colton parks, and I get out, following him up the pathway that is made of crumbling stone and weeds. He doesn't have to worry about the car being stolen around here as no one comes this far out, so he doesn't lock it. I climb up the old ladder that has bars around it to stop people falling, and pull myself onto the circular walkway near the top. I wait for Colton to climb up before we go and sit on the edge. Hooking my arms through the bars, I let my legs dangle off the side. I used to be scared of the height, but eventually, when I started to look around at the town and the lights, that fear dissipated. It's better not to let the fear of falling stop you from seeing the beauty of where you are.

"I like it when you watch the town; your whole face lights up," Colton tells me. I turn my head to look at him as he takes a piece of my brown hair in his fingers, twirling it gently before letting it fall.

"Colt," I whisper as he moves closer and pulls a box out of his pocket.

"It's your birthday gift. Well, the first one, and the second one, I'll have to give you tomorrow, as it's not done." I'm finding it hard to look away from him as he moves that bit closer to me.

"Oh. You didn't have to get me anything, but I'm not going to say no." I chuckle a little and accept the box. My eyes widen when I open it and see a bracelet inside. There are three silver crystals, shaped like roses, sitting in the middle of a silver bracelet.

"This is amazing, thank you so much," I tell him as he takes the bracelet out the box for me. I offer him my wrist, and he ties the bracelet then smiles at me.

"It's meant for you," he says, moving to brush a piece of my hair behind my ear. His face is so close to mine. When his finger trails down my cheek to my neck as we stare at each other, my breath hitches. Colt has never touched me like this before.

"What are we doing, Colt?" I ask him. He starts to answer when his phone rings. The phone ringing ruins the moment between us, and I move back. Colt swears under his breath as he gets his phone out of his pocket.

"Hello?" he answers as I lean back, and annoyance crosses his face.

"Yeah alright…alright…bye," he tells whoever is on the other end and then ends the call.

"I have to go, but I'll drive you home first. Can we meet up tomorrow? There's something I really need to tell you," Colt says.

"Should I worry?" I laugh, and he shakes his head with a sad look. He goes to say something, but his phone rings again. He takes a deep breath as he stands, pulling me up with him.

"Not at all," he smiles. Yet I can't seem to make myself believe him.

25

Harper

"One more drink. Come on, you're eighteen!" Skye shouts, clearly drunker than I am. She grins at me as I accept the small shot that can hardly be called a drink. I down it quickly, feeling the liquid burn my throat. It is my birthday, after all. Skye wanders off into the party, happy with herself that I've had a drink, and I'm relaxing a little. I look around the woods, seeing the huge fire in the middle of the clearing and my drunk classmates that surround it, dancing to the loud music. They clear as one guy I don't know kisses some random girl, and everyone cheers.

I watch as Skye talks to them all, and they laugh at whatever she says. I prefer to sit in the corner quietly, and I wish I could have brought my Kindle with me, but Skye wouldn't allow it. All she's cared about since I got here was where Colton was. He was right; I should have stayed at home or gone out with him, or something. This isn't what I would call fun, but I wanted to try what normal eighteen-year-olds are meant to be doing. My phone buzzes in my pocket, and I pull it out, seeing my foster mum's name flashing on the screen. I stand up, pulling my red coat closer around myself as I walk away from the party to answer the phone call.

"Harper, where are you?" she asks me straight away in her annoyed tone. I'm honestly surprised she's noticed I'm missing; she usually never does.

"I'm out with friends. It's my birthday," I say, not feeling the need to explain anything to her anymore. She made it clear last night, when she told me she isn't getting paid to have me anymore, she wants me out. I didn't get presents when I woke up; instead, I got told to make plans to find somewhere else to live. I don't know what I was expecting.

"You're not with that older boy, Colton?" she asks in an accusing tone.

"Colton is the same age as me, I've told you this millions of times, but no, he isn't here," I mutter. I don't know why, but she's convinced Colton is older than me when he isn't. It might have to do with how mature he is compared to most of the idiotic boys my age.

"I want you to come back home," she says, her voice quiet and extremely unlike the usual way she shouts at me. I keep walking through the woods as I think about what to say to her. Miss Linderale is the fourth foster parent I've had and, honestly, one of the nicer ones of the bunch. The rest are not worth thinking about.

"I don't get you. Why do you want me home? What changed from this morning?"

"Nothing. I wish I could keep you living with me, but I can't afford to, Harper. I thought you could come home, and we could look at local places for you to move to," she tells me, but I don't believe her for a second. Miss Linderale has a large three-bedroom house, and her husband works a good job. They have expensive things all around the house, and she never goes anywhere in any clothes that aren't designer. I know I should have applied to college, but I didn't have enough money or the grades because of moving all the time. You don't have time to study when you're packing your stuff or hiding from the new weird foster parents the social workers have found.

"Colton said I could move in with him and his family," I respond, disappointed, knowing some deep part of me just wants to be accepted by her.

"You cannot do that, Harper. You know how strange his family is. They never invite anyone over to their house," she says.

"I've been over once, they aren't that bad," I tell her, only lying a little bit. They are weird and cold, but it's not like they actually said anything bad towards me.

"Harper, just come home so we can talk. I'm not a heartless woman. I want you somewhere safe and with a planned future," she tells me.

"Sure, I'll come home soon," I say, kicking a rock with my foot and watching it fall down a hill. I stop walking when I realise how far I've gone, so far that I can't hear the party music anymore. I turn around in a circle, looking for the fire, and see it in the distance. I start walking back as Miss Linderale goes on about being responsible and saying that she's going to wait up for me.

"Do you understand, Harper?" she finishes.

"Yes, I'll see you in a bit," I say and end the call before she can lecture me anymore.

A deep, long growl comes from behind me, and I turn, my eyes widening at the sight of a big black wolf crouched down not far away from me. The wolf growls again and then turns, running into the forest.

"Wait!" I shout before I even think about what I just said. The wolf stops, looking over its shoulder at me as I step forward. It can't be a wolf; this is England, and we don't have wolves here, so it must be someone's pet. I don't want to get too close, but I should take a photo to put on the town Facebook page, in case someone lost him. I take another step closer, pulling out my phone and keeping eye contact with the wolf. I quickly glance down to open my camera. The growling gets louder, and I look up just in time to see the wolf running for me. I drop my phone and turn around, running as fast I can towards the party.

I shouldn't have done that. I can't believe how stupid I just was.

I scream when teeth clamp down on my leg and bite. I slam onto the ground, my chin smacking against the hard dirt. The wolf pulls on my leg, ripping my skin as I scream and try to kick him off. It doesn't work, and everything is going blurry as pain racks through my leg. The ache consumes every thought as I reach down and try to push the wolf's head away from my leg. All I can see is the blood on my hands and all over its face, mixing with its black fur and white sharp teeth. It's going to kill me.

"Help!" I shout, my words quieter than I want them to be. Nothing makes sense as the wolf shakes my leg and pain causes the words to choke in my mouth. As everything starts to go black and the forest disappears, I see a grey wolf running towards me through the trees. Its terrifying growl is the last thing I hear.

26

Colton

"*H*arper, answer your damn phone," I mutter as her phone rings and then goes to voicemail. I look around my bedroom, settling on the glass of blood on the side table, and feel my teeth respond. I down the drink as I wait for the stupid beep. I run my hand through my hair, not even knowing what to say. I've already left her ten messages.

"I don't know where you are, but I know you didn't come home after the party. I called Skye, who said you walked off. I'm getting worried now. Call me back," I say and put the phone down. I first went to her foster parents' this morning, and her foster mom said she moved out. I don't trust her as far as I can throw her.

Harper wouldn't just disappear like that without saying something to me. Plus, she has nowhere to go. I walk out of my bedroom, stopping when I see my sister, Belle, talking to my other sister, Light, in the corridor. Belle is kneeling down, as Light is only eight and tiny. Both my sisters have the same colour blonde hair, like mine. Both very pretty, and I know I will have trouble protecting Light when she is as old as Belle and has men chasing after her. Luckily for my dad and me, Belle isn't interested in dating and turns every man down. It's almost funny to see the same reaction from every guy.

"What was the bad dream about?" Belle asks Light.

"Wolves. A wolf bit a girl, and then there was a war. A bad war, and you—" Light starts. As I step closer, she stops talking, giving me a sad little smile. I don't know what to say to her; Belle is the best with her, out of all of us. Light isn't my biological sister, but she is a vampire, and she lives in our coven as my parents adopted her as a baby when she had no one left. The ten blue stars in a circular mark in the middle of her forehead puts her at risk.

"It's just a dream, it's not real," Belle tells her

and then stands up. "Why don't we go and make some of that fried chicken you like?"

"Okay," Light replies, and they walk down the stairs. I try to ring Harper once again as I let myself out of the house and get into my SUV. I hate that I can't be with her at night, not until I can explain everything, and now this happens. It would freak her out to see my extended sharp teeth and glowing purple eyes. She is human, after all.

"Where are you going?" Belle asks, stopping next to my window, having run impossibly fast to the side of my Land Rover. I roll my window down, and she leans in, her long blonde hair sweeping the ledge. Her eyes, the same colour as mine, are hard to look at. She knows I'm worried.

"To find Harper. She isn't answering her phone, and that's not like her," I say.

"The human," Belle tuts. Belle hates humans and wolves and, well, everyone that isn't her. Except for Light, who grows at a normal human rate until she turns eighteen and has made Belle fall in love with her. I want to blame Belle and tell her to be less harsh to people, but she had a bad past.

"She is my destined mate, Belle. Mine. I knew

it was her when I first saw her, but I was more certain than ever yesterday, on her eighteenth birthday. What went from a slight desire and a need to be close to her and protect her, turned to actual pain in my chest from being away from her. I will go mad if I lose her now, I can't," I reply.

"Okay, okay, chill...but I still think you can do better than her," she says and stands back as I glare at her.

"You have never met your mate. You wouldn't be able to understand," I tell her, and she just shakes her head at me. Belle is my sister, but there are one hundred years between us, which makes her think she knows everything. Belle doesn't know anything about Harper because she never tried to get to know her. I haven't even told Harper about my siblings yet because I know she would want to meet them, and they wouldn't behave.

"One more thing. There were rogue hunters in town last night," she says, and I groan. That's not a good sign. If hunters were here, then a rogue would have been in town. Rogues have no control of their wolves; they are basically wild animals. It's like a vampire who doesn't feed for three weeks—they go feral, attacking anything or anyone.

I drive to where the party in the woods took place the night before, parking next to the bottles of beer and rubbish that are surrounding a deserted campfire. It takes me a few minutes to track Harper's scent, and I run fast through the woods towards where the scent is strongest. I stop when I see the blood; there's so much blood. I can smell that it's not all Harper's, that some of it belongs to a wolf. The rogue must have attacked her, but I don't see her or her body anywhere. I feel sick as I pull my phone out.

"Dad, I need your help. I need you to use your powers to find Harper," I beg. My dad can track anyone, and he only needs to meet them once. My father is an exception to the rules, a turned vampire with a gift. He once worked for the vampire royal family; now, he is retired, in a way. Or retired to protect Light, as he was the one who found her on the doorsteps of the royal castle as a newborn baby.

"Harper?" he asks, knowing I would never ask him for anything unless I had no choice.

"Yes, I think she's hurt," I say.

"I can see her in a car with wolves. The

wolves have a bag that says the Forest pack on it," my dad says eventually. "Be careful, the wolves won't give her up easily," he warns.

"Thank you," I reply, and end the call before he can try to convince me not to go after her. I run back to my car as I search the pack on the supernaturals website and see that it's a large pack in Ireland.

"Seems like I'm rescuing my destined mate from some wolves," I mutter, as I get in the car and start the engine.

How far can fate make you fall?

When Adelaide turned twenty, losing her parents and gaining custody of her fifteen-year-old sister were not part of her plan.

If being a shifter in a world where her kind is hunted wasn't bad enough, she now has to protect her sister too. Adie has no choice but to move into the old house her parents left them, or risk being on the streets in a dangerous world.

Only she didn't expect to be living next door to a strange, and very attractive, group of men who are far more than human.

They offer her protection in exchange for keeping their reason for hiding from the humans a secret and helping them. But protection comes at a cost, and the cost is something none of them could have expected.

A cost that's been destined. A cost that fate has weaved for Adelaide. A cost that even princes cannot escape.

(Her Guardians series spin-off)

Reverse Harem

17 +

Prologue

"*R*un faster," the breathless voice of my mate's best friend shouts to me as I rush through the cold woods in Scotland where we planned to escape to. At least our information on the portal was right. The freezing wind hits my face as snow brushes against my bare legs, making me want to fall into the snow and give up. I fight the cold, unforgiving snow for as long as I can. Keeping the image of my mate in my mind. He would never give up.

"I can't," I say, collapsing to the ground as pain rips through my stomach. I look down as blood coats the snow-covered floor by my stomach. I can't do this anymore, it's too late, and I can feel the poison spreading through my body from the dagger.

"Reni," I whisper my companion's name as she slides to her knees in front of me, my gaze goes to my newborn daughter that she holds in blankets close to her chest. Two hours, that's all I had with her before they attacked us. *It's not enough.*

"I will stay and fight to protect you, for him," Reni says sharply, handing me my daughter, and I push her away gently, my heart breaking as she cries.

"No, go. It's too late, and I can't outrun them. I can distract them enough by closing the last portal," I say quietly as Reni's eyes widen in shock. If I close that portal, then there is no way for her and her army to follow us.

"Using any power now will kill you. My alpha died to keep you alive. You can't do this to me," she begs me, keeping her voice in a whisper for the baby. I look around the snow-covered forest, remembering the Autumn court and the brief happiness I felt there when I married the man I loved and had my beautiful daughter. The Autumn court was always home and where I expected I would die one day. Now I'm going to die in Winter, on Earth, of all worlds. So very far from home.

"Something is wrong, and neither of us are healers. Take my child and keep her safe. Please," I say reaching to hold a hand against my sleeping child wrapped in her arms. I twirl a finger around the dark red hair on her head, the same colour as mine and all the royal family before me. Her bright green eyes watch me, and she doesn't make a sound. She is so innocent for the world she has been born into. Reni looks down at me and then to my little baby she holds in her arms.

"I will do it for you. I will do it for my lost alpha and my queen. I will bring her up with my mate as our own. No one will know who she is," Reni says, finally giving in, and I know her well enough to know she means every word. She may not be Fray, but she is family to me.

"Her name is Adelaide, after my mother," I tell Reni gently, who nods.

"That name will give her identity away on Frayan," Reni reminds me what I already know. It is a royal Frayan name. No common Fray could name their child it. It would be highly disrespectful. Not that it matters. Once she stepped into

Fray, everything about her would give her identity away.

"No one can know who she is. You must keep her away from anything Fray-touched. She must never get her Fray powers or wings," I tell her, knowing that there is no way she can be taken back to Frayan. When I close the portal, it will be impossible, but there are weapons here that have Fray magic, even some creatures that have passed through portals. They won't have enough magic to reveal her powers, but over time...they would make them appear.

"You have my word. I'm sorry I can't save you," she says with tears running down her face. Everything starts going blurry as she stands and offers me a hand to help me up. I stand shakily and look down once more at Adelaide before turning away, my heart breaking. *I have to do this.*

"They are coming, go," I say, and she nods holding my daughter closer.

"I'm sorry," she bows the best she can when holding a baby. My mind flashes back to the prophecy surrounding my child and the Fray courts that have fallen to keep her safe. She has to be safe. I watch until I can't see Reni anymore before walking back off into the woods. When I see the portal, a slightly blue clear shimmer that only Fray can see, I lift my hands. It only takes a second for my lightening power to shoot purple bolts of lightning out my hands into the portal. My wings flutter behind me, lifting me slightly into the air as my power gets stronger. The portal cracks slowly, bit by bit until it explodes, and I go flying into the air. I close my eyes and think only of Adelaide, knowing she will be safe, as darkness takes me.

Chapter 27

"Adie, why do we have to move? The old house was fine," my little sister says as she groans from her seat next to me in my small car. The car that somehow seems smaller every time she asks me the same question. *Shitadoodle, what do I tell her?* I look over at Sophie, who is sat with one ear plug in and doesn't take her eyes off her tablet as she waits for an answer I don't want to give her. I can't worry my fifteen-year-old sister with the facts about our money situation, and the fact we have absolutely none. The truth of the matter is that our parents liked to travel around all the time, and that wasn't good for keeping a long-term job. All the traveling meant that when they died two months ago, in a car crash, I had to sell our house to pay off our debts and then move my sister into the house left in the will. I look out at the snow and ice on the road, deciding I'm not going to like this small town. Well it's not that bad, as Scotland isn't too far away and remote. The new house is only seven hours' drive away from York, where I was at university. *Deep breath, and answer her, Adelaide.*

"Adie," Sophie sighs louder than before, and I put my foot on the gas a little more and pray my piece of crap car will actually get us to the house. God knows I don't have the money to pay for a pickup truck or any idea who to call. The old Peugeot is traveling way too far than I would have ever trusted it to, but I really can't afford to pay for a new car.

"We are nearly there," I finally say. That was a lame answer, and I know it.

"Great," she huffs, and I just catch her rolling her eyes at me from under her brown hair before she goes back to whatever game she is playing on her tablet.

"I know this is a big change, but it will be good for us," I tell her as she finally looks at me for a second before huffing in response, again, and going back on her tablet. Sophie used to be a chatty twelve-year-old who loved sports. Or at least that's what I remember her being like when I left for university, but now she is a shell of herself since our parents' death. My heart drops as I remember that they are really gone, and I have a teenager to look after, with no job and hardly any money. I haven't had time to grieve because I can't melt down in front of Sophie. It's going to be difficult enough to find work that works around Sophie in a small town. A university dropout isn't a good person to hire. I had no choice but to leave when the accident happened; I couldn't move Sophie into my shared dorm at university with what the world is like now. *They would kill her and me for one slip-up.* The small village finally comes into view after over an hour of driving down an empty country lane. The village is near enough to a big town, so I can drive there to work in the day, and it apparently has a very good school that I've gotten Sophie into. She doesn't start for a few weeks though, and considering we can hardly talk to each other, the idea of being stuck in an old house for weeks is not appealing.

It takes me a few wrong turns down empty roads until I find a row of four houses. Our house is the last of the attached houses, and it has its own driveway that I pull up in. Sophie finally looks up from her iPad and frowns at the sight of the overgrown lawn and old paint falling off the outside of the old house. *Home, sweet, home.* The house looks close to falling apart, and it takes everything in me not to slam my head against the steering wheel at the sight. The estate agent said it was in good order, this isn't what I thought it would be like. I wrench my door open, muttering "fuck" to myself as I slam it shut behind me and go up the two steps to the door. Thankfully the locks look new, kind of, and the door opens easily before I walk in.

The smell of dust is the first thing that hits me as I look around at the hallway, which has cobwebs in every corner, and it is empty of any decorations. The space isn't too bad I guess, and it is painted in a light brown which matches the wooden floors. There are three dark wooden doors, one at the end and one on each side of the hall. I open the first one to a small empty room which I'm guessing is a storage closet or study. The next room is a lounge with a large fireplace, two covered sofas, and a small coffee table. This room isn't too bad. I go to the window and open the thick cream curtains, coughing from the dust and pushing the window open to let some air in here. I pull the white sheets off both sofas, and they are brown like the colour all the rooms have been painted in, by the looks of it so far.

I leave the lounge and go to the door at the end of corridor, opening it up to find a kitchen. The kitchen is a similar brown to the walls, with dark wooden counters, and I thank god when I see there's a working fridge and cooker that just need plugging in. After a little moving things around, nearly dying from inhaling more dust, I manage to get them turned on. I open the window in the kitchen, letting some more much needed air in. I am going to be up all night cleaning this house from dust and cobwebs. When I come back to the door to get some boxes, Sophie is walking up the stairs, and shouts down from the top, just as I grab the handle.

"The beds don't look bad. Bring me some of my stuff up, won't you?" she shouts, and I groan internally while pulling the door open and shuffling my feet back to the car. When did she get so damn bossy? Can I even tell her off for it after we lost mum and dad? I'm no parent to her. Sophie and I have never been the closest of sisters. We argue more than get along, but now everything has changed, and I don't know where I stand with her. I shake my head, knowing I can't overthink this, and I need to just take one day at a time. I'm so lost in my thoughts, that I don't look where I am going at all. The next thing I know, I trip over what I assume is a large rock in the middle of the driveway and brace myself for the hard fall I'm going to suffer. Somehow that doesn't happen; instead, I feel a warm chest against my back and strong big arms wrapped around my stomach as someone catches me. I turn my head to thank whoever it is, and my breath catches. The hottest guy I've ever seen is staring at me with sparking clear blue eyes. His dark brown hair is short on the sides with an overgrown fringe which has blond tips, and he has a five o'clock shadow. I have to blink a few times to find out if he is real, because men don't look like this. No, only gods do, I imagine.

"I don't usually have girls fall for me without knowing their name," he says, a casual smirk on his lips as I stare speechless at him. *They don't make men like this in Britain, or anywhere, so where the hell did he come from?* I reluctantly pull out of his arms and move to stand in front of him. He is really tall, as I have to stretch my neck to look up to see his face. I'm not that short, but this guy must be well over six foot.

"I'm Adie," I hold out a hand, and he slides his slightly cold hand into mine. The man gives me a slight, deep sexy chuckle as he turns my hand over in his before pulling it up to his lips for a gentle kiss. The moment his lips touch my skin, I feel a shock, that's the only way to explain it, and by his widened eyes, I know he feels it too. I pull my hand away quickly, and my body takes a step back before I even realise it. I don't know what the hell that was, but my hand is still somewhat tingling from the contact.

"It is nice to meet you, Adie. I'm Rick. My brother and I live there," he points to the house next door to mine, "with our two friends." I internally sigh at the fact I have to live next to the hottie who no doubt knows his way around women, and I know I will be drooling over him for the considerable future. Not that a guy like this would be interested in me. I have hips, no boobs to be seen anywhere, and I'm a twenty-year-old virgin. I'm way out of my league with this guy. Not that it matters. The last thing I need right now is any distractions from looking after Sophie. Holy hotness, this means I have to live next to four guys who might all be as hot as this dude, and somehow keep focused. I can only hope they mow the lawn shirtless once in a while. *That would be awesome to see.*

"Adie, where are you? If you are going to take this long, I'll get my own stuff," Sophie's unimpressed voice comes from the door, and I turn to see her just stop when she sees I'm talking to someone. Her eyes watch Rick carefully, and I have to clear my throat to get her attention and to stop her from doing something crazy like be territorial and growl at the human guy.

"This is my sister, Sophie. Sophie, this is one of our new neighbours, Rick," I introduce them as Sophie walks over to us, stopping at my side. Rick holds a hand out to Sophie, who looks at the hand in disgust before ignoring him completely by going around us to the car.

"I'm sorry about her," I say as my cheeks go red at Sophie's behaviour. I watch her open the boot and start pulling out boxes, putting them down as she looks for her bag.

"No problem. I know what it is like to be an angry kid. Do you want some help with the boxes?" Rick asks me, and I glance up at him. He is smiling, no sign of him being angry or not understanding, and in fact, there is sympathy etched across his features.

"If you're not busy," I find myself replying, even though it is dangerous to make friends with any humans when we need to be invisible in this village. Though he hasn't noticed how my teenage sister is lifting very heavy boxes out of the boot like they are pillows, so we might be okay. I can just let him help with the boxes and then make an excuse so he has to leave. Nice and simple.

"Nope. It's my day off work, and I literally have nothing to do," he tells me with a big grin. I laugh as he goes to the car just as Sophie walks past with her large backpack, flashing Rick a glare which he thankfully ignores. Part of me wants to tell her off for being rude, but her eyes look watery, and so much has changed for her that I can't help but feel sorry for her. This can't be easy. I pat her shoulder as she goes by, and she nudges me away in clear anger. I swallow the hurt as I watch her run into the house before I go to grab a box. I get to the back of the car just as Rick picks up three boxes like they weigh nothing. The boxes have kitchen written on the side of them, so I know they are filled with heavy plates and kitchen things. I don't say anything as I follow Rick in with my one box. I could have grabbed three or more like he did, but that might give away my secret, and my parents taught me better than that growing up. Learning to pretend how to be human is something built into my bones at this point. It's Sophie I worry about. There were several times we had to run and leave everything because she forgot how deadly it is for humans to know what we are.

"Wow, you must work out," I say as we put the boxes on the floor in the kitchen, and I carry one of them into the lounge.

"Sometimes," he mutters behind me, and I look back to see him watching me strangely or something, before leaving the house for more boxes, I guess. I forget the look, following him out after putting my box down, and together we get them all in the house with little trouble.

"Thanks for all your help, can I ask where the local store is?" I ask, noting that it's getting dark, and I need to get some food for Sophie and me to eat tonight. "Actually, don't worry, I will just Google it."

"The store closes soon, so it's pointless to go now. I will order pizza. The pizza shop is literally five minutes away, and I'm a regular," he winks at me, and then pulls his phone out, calling for pizza without waiting for my reply.

"Ah thanks. A takeout would be good for the first night," I say, grabbing my bag off one of the boxes in the lounge. Rick follows me in, chatting on the phone to the pizza man like they are best friends.

"Put the money away, it's on me. Any preferred toppings?" he asks, and I shake my head, putting my purse back. Judging from his slightly demanding tone, he isn't going to let me pay.

"Surprise me," I reply, my voice more husky than usual, and I swiftly realise that I'm flirting. I quickly look away, reminding myself that this man is a human and out of my league. *Jesus, control yourself, Adie.* It's been like an hour, and I'm already flirting and forgetting everything my parents told me. *Get it together, Adie, you can't flirt with humans anyway. Wolves and humans don't date, everyone knows that.*

I leave him to order and take a box of Sophie's stuff up the stairs. It's a pretty basic house with a small bathroom in the middle and two rooms on either side, which is just like the photos of the house in the will. But the photos made it look much nicer than it is. I follow the only light on to the room on the left, the one Sophie must have claimed. The door is slightly open, so I can see that Sophie is sat on a chair in the one room with her iPad and doesn't notice me come in. I place the box on the floor by the door, looking around the simple room. There is a double bed with a mattress, and Sophie has made up her bed with her purple sheets. The wardrobe is open, and she has even started to put clothes away before getting bored I suspect. I'm just glad it isn't that dusty in here.

"Soph, Rick is ordering pizza. Will you come and eat with us?" I ask gently, and she finally looks up at me. I see straight away that she has been crying, and it's heartbreaking to see her like this. I walk over and pull her into a hug even as she protests by trying to push me away. "You don't have to be strong around me. I miss them too. I'm sad too, and there is no one that understands what you are feeling like I do."

"I miss them so much," she cries, relaxing into my hug as I look down at her iPad and the photo of mum and dad on it. They are both smiling in front of a tent, with Sophie right in the middle of them, a big goofy grin on her face and one tooth missing because she fell out of a tree the day before, knocking it out. Luckily, it was only a baby tooth that hadn't fallen out yet. I remember taking this photo years ago when we went camping. Like we did every year because it was the only safe place to shift and run together as a pack. It doesn't even seem real that they are gone, and we will never get to do that again. I hold Sophie tighter to me, so grateful that at least she is alive and didn't get into the car that night. If I had lost her as well…I can't even imagine losing her.

"I miss them more than I could ever describe, but I want you to know I'm here. You always have a home with me. I'm not mum or dad, and I'm crap at knowing what is best, but I am going to try my best to make this work," I tell her firmly, because I mean every word.

"Thanks, Adie. You're the best sister. I'm sorry I'm a little shit at times," she sniffles.

"Mum would threaten to wash your mouth out with soap if she heard you say 'shit'," I joke, and it seems to lighten the mood as she smiles at me.

"I know, but she said 'shit' a lot. Just usually under her breath when she dropped something or was mad at dad, but she would usually add 'head' to that one," Sophie says, and we both laugh as she pulls away. It hurts to look at Sophie sometimes because she looks so much like mum, her brown hair is the same dark colour, and she has her brown eyes too. It just reminds me how much I do not look like my sister or my parents.

"So, pizza?" I ask, reminding myself why I came up here in the first place and that Rick is waiting downstairs.

"Sure. Call me down when it gets here, please," she replies.

I kiss the side of Sophie's head before walking out of her room and pause in the hallway, staring at the full length mirror that is half covered up by a blanket. I pull the blanket off and stare at myself for a second. In some ways, it is good that I don't look like Sophie or my mum because I don't remind myself of mum. Mum was willowy thin, with thin brown hair and dark brown eyes. Dad was similar looking, but in a more geeky way when mum was more delicate. I twirl a bit of my dark red hair around my finger, which is thick and wavy down to my waist. My hair isn't a tiny bit thin, it is thick and uncontrollable at the best of times. My bright green eyes shine back at me, the green complements my shiny red hair.

Whereas my parents had dark tanned skin like Sophie, mine is pale, and no matter how much I sun tan, it sure doesn't change. My hips make my shirt rise a little, revealing a little bit of skin, and I pull my shirt down to cover it. I know I shouldn't have eaten that second chocolate muffin at the garage we stopped at, but at the time, I didn't feel a tiny bit guilty. I think back to the conversation I had with my mum once about why I look so much different than them, and I asked if I was adopted or something as a joke. Mum just snapped that I looked like her brother and then left the room like her ass was on fire. I always wished I had asked her more, and for pictures of her brother, but it's too late now. I shake my head, stepping back and hanging the sheet over the railing on the stairs. I know it's just moving into this new home and losing my parents that is making me feel like this. I just need to relax for a bit. I run down the stairs, walking into the lounge.

"Everything ok?" Rick asks me from where he is sat on the sofa, looking comfy with his feet on the coffee table.

"Yeah. I don't know if Sophie will come down, but she might do," I reply, feeling awkward.

"It's been a rough few months, and she is only fifteen. I know she is sorry about earlier."

"Is she your sister?" he asks with clear questions in his eyes. He must be wondering how a twenty-year-old, or however old he thinks I am, is looking after a fifteen-year-old alone.

"Yes. Our parents passed away a few months ago," I say quietly as my voice still catches as I admit it.

"I'm sorry, I know what it's like to lose your mother, but mine was when I was a lot younger. I have a stepmum anyway, so I was lucky. Hell, I'm not making this any better, am I?" he asks me, rapidly speaking like he is nervous, and we both chuckle.

"Then I'm sorry about your loss too," I comment, and he nods.

"So…what brings you to Midview village, i.e. the land of the boring old people," he asks, leaning back and grinning at me. Whatever nervousness he had is lost, and he's back to being charming, which is somehow making me nervous.

"My parents owned this house and not much else. I thought it would be a good place to start," I say, and he nods.

"Our reasons are similar apparently. We all

needed a new start too, and this place had the perfect job. At least for now," he says, and then suddenly goes serious as he leans forward, placing his hands on his knees.

"When were you going to tell me that you're a shifter? And while you're at it, why the hell are you really here?"

Chapter 28

*M*y heart must be banging a million miles a minute as I watch Rick's eyes glow like mine in the dimly lit room. A growl escapes my lips as he finally stops hiding his wolf, and its presence overwhelms mine—he is powerful. *An alpha. How did he hide?*

"How did you appear so human to me?" I ask, my words coming out as more of a growl as my wolf pushes me to shift and challenge Rick in order to protect Sophie. Rick stands up, and I do the same, keeping still and refusing to back down. I hold his gaze, knowing it is never smart to run from a wolf. Let alone an alpha wolf. Though I've never run from my own kind before, it's just what my mum always told me.

"A gift of mine, but I won't hurt you," he says moving closer to me, holding his hands up, and I can't feel any kind of threat coming from him. I don't know if he is telling me the truth, but when he takes another step closer, I let out a long growl, and I almost let my wolf take over. He does pause though, not pushing me any further, which surprises me a little, but my growl must have caused Sophie to panic, as the next thing I see is a brown bundle slam into Rick's chest. It knocks him over, and he hits the sofa as he falls. I rush to pull Sophie off him, but a long growl from Rick stops me. He slowly stands up, holding Sophie as she tries to bite him and claw at his shirt, ripping it in places.

"Sophie," I plead as Rick picks her up by the scruff on her neck, holding her away from him, and she whines in annoyance.

"That was unexpected," Rick grunts, looking down at his shirt. "I loved this damn shirt, pup."

"Don't hurt her," I beg, moving slowly closer to them as panic fills me until I can't stop shaking. I'm a little shocked when Rick softly places Sophie into my arms. Sophie licks my chin as I look down at her, checking she is okay even though I know she is.

"You shouldn't attack an alpha, pup," Rick laughs, and his big hand strokes her head. I'm surprised when she happily lets him fuss her. "I used to challenge my uncle when I was a pup, until I learnt it wasn't a good idea until I got older and stood at least a little bit of a chance."

"I've never met another wolf, other than our parents. Neither has Sophie, and our parents were not alphas," I tell him, and he frowns briefly, going to say something, but a door slams open, and a man walks in the open lounge doorway. The man smells human, but everything from the way he stands to the way he stares at me like he is planning my death tells me he is anything but. Sophie whines as I place her behind me on the sofa and move in front of her with a growl at the man whose gaze darkens. The man has wavy black hair that curls away from his face, revealing his dark blue eyes. They are so dark, you can only just see the blue, and without staring like I did, you would think they were just black. The man keeps his hands at his side, tightly in fists, and his muscular arms press against his black leather jacket.

"What the fuck is going on, Rick?" he asks in a

deadly calm voice, which is somehow seductive. It sounds like a voice that could talk you into dying for him without saying much more than a whisper. Even though he asks Rick the question, his eyes still watch my every move. Assessing everything about me, I bet. I run my eyes over him, having the feeling he is not a wolf, he seems too deadly for that. Everything about him sends shivers and warning bells through me, yet I can't seem to pull my gaze away.

"Josh, we have new neighbours. Two wolves who have no pack and are clearly in hiding," Rick says, maneuvering himself so he is in front of me and cutting my gaze from Josh off. I move to the side, not wanting to be blocked, and Josh only smirks at the action.

"Then send them to the castle before anyone notices," Josh retorts. "*She* needs to fucking leave."

"I'm not going anywhere, but why don't you get the hell out of my house before I make you," I suggest, crossing my arms and keeping my head high. "Get out."

"You have no idea who you are taking to, sweetheart," the man growls, a light blue shimmer appearing all over his skin as he reveals the massive black wings on his back. *Angel. A dark one.* I growl low until Rick moves in front of me, blocking my view of Josh again.

"Leave, Josh. I will figure out who they are, but I don't sense a threat here. You need to calm the fuck down," Rick warns, a low growl slipping out with his words. "Calm it down now or we need to take this outside, and I don't want to fight you again, bro."

"I am calm, brother," Josh replies smoothly, though his gravelly voice suggests otherwise.

"Josh…" Rick warns him again, this time his words are filled with an alpha demand. It's enough to make me shiver and want to fall to my knees in submission, but I fight it off. *I won't submit to anyone.* I glance back at Sophie, whose wolf has submitted in a heartbeat and is rolled onto her back, showing her stomach off. It would usually make me chuckle, if it were in a different circumstance, that is.

"Fine," Josh responds, and I glance around Rick just in time to see Josh walk out the door, leaving it open behind him. The sound of the front door opening and shutting is heard not long after. There's an awkward silence as Rick turns around, lifting a massive, muscular arm and rubbing the back of his head.

"You might want to stay away from Josh…he won't hurt you, but he doesn't like strangers. Especially not right now," Rick says, defending his brother.

"Got it. Stay away from tall, dark and downright terrifying is something I can do," I mutter and turn around, picking Sophie up. I walk her to the stairs and place her on the bottom one. "Run to your room and change back. We are safe, I just need to talk to Rick alone." Sophie whines, pressing her head against my hand before running up the stairs like I asked her to.

"Why are you here?" Rick asks me, and I turn around to see him leaning against the door frame like a model for a magazine. I go to answer when the front door bell rings, and Rick goes to answer it. I can smell the pizza from here, without even opening the door.

"Go and sit, it's the pizza," he tells me, holding the door handle as I pause, not knowing if I can trust him. "I promise that I will never hurt you. I only want to talk and understand why you are here without a pack." I don't answer him, but

I do walk into the lounge and awkwardly sit on the sofa. Rick comes back in the room not long after and slides the pizza on the coffee table, opening it up.

"I would get plates, but everything is in boxes," I say, reaching across and breaking a piece off as Rick sits on the other sofa with his own piece.

"You don't need plates for pizza," Rick says, shrugging his massive shoulders, and I agree. We eat silently, to the point that it is seriously uncomfortable.

"What do you want to know?" I ask when I have finished my slice, and Rick has already finished his and had a second one as he eats super quickly. He spreads his arms back across the top of the sofas and watches me closely.

"Where is your pack?" he asks. "What is their name, and why are they not protecting two young females?"

"We don't have a pack. My mum and dad said there were no packs around anymore, none that could be trusted anyways. We kept moving to keep safe," I explain, and he looks confused as he processes my answer for a few seconds.

"That's not true, Red," Rick mutters. "There are plenty of packs that protect their own, and until ten years ago, they were spread all around the world."

"I don't know why my parents didn't go to any, but they always kept us hidden and moving around. What happened in Paris...well we had to keep super low down after that," I say, referring to how Paris suddenly had a massive ward appear all around it for months. When the ward came down, most of the people in Paris were missing or dead. And some of the people had turned into things almost like zombies. It soon came out that supernaturals were real and had caused what happened in Paris. After that, anything different or suspected as supernatural was hunted and usually killed. Everywhere in the world suddenly became extremely dangerous overnight for people like my family.

"Coming here is not keeping you safe. You need protection, an alpha and a pack," Rick mutters angrily. "Your parents risked your life way too much by hiding you."

"Why? We have done fine without one. My parents clearly kept us alive and fine," I remark, folding my arms in annoyance, and he huffs, shaking his head.

"The world is dangerous for supernaturals. Hunters are everywhere and actively hunting anyone different," he tells me what I already know.

"I know that. We are good at hiding, and this village is tiny, no one will look for us here," I retort. It's not like I moved into the middle of London where I couldn't shift and would be found super easily.

"This village is not what it seems. You need to leave," Rick says gently, but it is firm and a demand.

"We have nowhere to go. I had to drop out of university, I have no job, and this house was all that was left in my parents' will," I admit to him. "I couldn't sell this house if I tried, and I have to do what is best for Sophie."

"Shit," Rick grumbles, rubbing his face. "Then I guess I will look after you for a week. We have a place I can get you to, and you will be safe. You will be with your own kind."

"There is nowhere safe," I remark, not understanding where he thinks I can just go to.

"I grew up in the safest place for supernaturals, and my stepmum is the queen of the supernaturals. Winter will give you both a home and protect you. She does that for anyone that needs help," he explains to me. I stare at him for a second in shock. There is a queen of the supernaturals and somewhere safe to live? Sounds like a fairy tale. If Rick's stepmum is queen, then he must be a prince. Just my luck to trip over and literally be caught by Prince Charming.

"I don't know…" I let my voice drift off.

"I'm not living here for no reason, and this village is more dangerous than anywhere else. Let me help you," he asks. "I want to help you."

"Now I think about it, I've heard rumours of the supernaturals having a queen and four kings. That they hide all the supernaturals with them. It was a story told around university," I reply, being honest with him. "It always sounded like a fairy tale that couldn't be true. My parents said it must be lies, and I really didn't think on it until now."

"Not one part of it is a lie. I am prince, heir to the supernatural throne, and I promise on my blood to protect you," he says, and goose bumps spread all over my skin as we stare at each other. "You are my pack, and as your alpha now, I will keep you safe no matter what." The more I stare at Rick, I get the feeling he isn't joking one bit, and what he did was very serious.

"Rick, look, how can I believe you?" I ask, standing up and resisting the urge to pace as I keep eye contact with him. I won't drop my gaze, not when I know he is an alpha, and my wolf wouldn't let me anyway. I've never been a submissive wolf. My parents once submitted to me when I was mad about something silly. I just didn't know I was an alpha female until then. Mum and dad said alpha wolves are rare and meant to be more powerful than usual wolves. They are meant to lead. The only place I would lead anyone is into trouble, so that can't be true.

"That's the thing, you already do trust me, but you don't know *why* you trust me," he says, grinning as he stands up and walks to the door. "Come over to our house and meet the others in the morning. They will want to meet you, and we need to sort out a way to make you seem human."

"Are they as scary as Josh?" I ask quietly, not wanting to touch the subject about how I trust this hottie already. I'm sure it's just a wolf thing and nothing to do with how damn sexy, protective and stunning he is. Rick laughs, and I resist the urge to shiver at how nice his laugh sounds.

"No one is as scary as Josh," he winks at me, and walks out the room. I wait for the front door to shut before collapsing back on the sofa, not having a clue if I am right for trusting the handsome next door neighbour. *Or if I just made a big mistake.*